Gustave Aimard

Stronghand

Vol. I

SALZWASSER
VERLAG

Gustave Aimard

Stronghand

Vol. I

Reprint of the original, first published in 1863.

1st Edition 2022 | ISBN: 978-3-37500-201-5

Verlag (Publisher): Salzwasser Verlag GmbH, Zeilweg 44, 60439 Frankfurt, Deutschland
Vertretungsberechtigt (Authorized to represent): E. Roepke, Zeilweg 44, 60439 Frankfurt, Deutschland
Druck (Print): Books on Demand GmbH, In de Tarpen 42, 22848 Norderstedt, Deutschland

STRONGHAND

OR

THE NOBLE REVENGE

A Tale of the Disinherited

By GUSTAVE AIMARD

IN TWO VOLUMES

VOL. I

LONDON

MDCCCLXIII

CONTENTS OF VOL. I.

STRONGHAND.

CHAPTER I.

AN EXCHANGE OF SHOTS.

The country extending between the Sierra de San Saba and the Rio Puerco, or Dirty River, is one of the most mournful and melancholy regions imaginable.

This accursed savannah, on which bleach unrecognised skeletons, which the wind and sun strive to convert into dust, is an immense desert, broadcast with grey rocks, beneath which snakes and wild beasts have, from time immemorial, formed their lurking-place, and which only produces black shrubs and stunted larches that rise from distance to distance above the desert.

White or Indian travellers rarely and most unwillingly venture to cross this frightful solitude, and at the risk of lengthening their journey they prefer making a detour and following the border, where they are certain of finding shade and water—those delights of tropical countries and indispensable necessities for a long trip on the western prairies.

Toward the second half of June—which the Navajoe Indians call the "strawberry moon" in their harmonious language—and in the Year of Grace 1843, a horseman suddenly emerged from a thick clump of oaks, sumachs, and mahogany trees, entered the savannah at a gallop, and, instead of following the usual travellers' track which was distinctly traced on the edge of the sand, he began without any hesitation crossing the desert in a straight line.

This resolution was a mark of great folly, or a proof of extraordinary daring on the part of a solitary man, however brave he might be; or else some imperious reasons compelled him to lay aside all prudence in order to reach his journey's end more speedily.

However, whatever the motives that might determine the traveller, he continued his journey rapidly, and buried himself deeper and deeper in the desert, without seeming to notice the gloomy and desolate aspect the landscape around him constantly assumed.

As this person is destined to play an important part in our story, we will draw his portrait in a few words. He was a man of from twenty-five to thirty years of age—belonging to the pure Mexican race, of average height, and possessed of elegant manners; while his every gesture, graceful though it was, revealed a far from ordinary strength. His face, with its regular features and bright hue, evidenced frankness, bravery, and kindliness; his black eyes, haughty and well open, had a straight and penetrating glance; his well-cut mouth, adorned with dazzling white teeth, was half concealed beneath a long brown moustache; his chin, of too marked an outline perhaps, denoted a great firmness of character; in short, his whole appearance aroused interest and attracted sympathy.

As for his dress, it was the Mexican costume in all its picturesque richness. His broad-brimmed Vicuna skin hat, decorated with a double gold and silver *golilla*, was carelessly set on his right ear, and allowed curls of luxurious black hair to fall in disorder on his shoulders. He wore a jacket of green velvet, magnificently embroidered with gold, under which could be seen a worked linen shirt. An Indian handkerchief was fastened round his neck by a diamond ring. His *calzoneras*, also of green velvet, held round his hips by a red silk gold-fringed *fa-ja*, were embroidered and slashed like a jacket, while two rows of pearl-set gold buttons ran along the opening that extends from the boot to the knee. His vaquera boots, embroidered with pretty designs in red thread, were fastened to his legs by silk-and-gold garters, from one of which emerged the admirably-carved hilt of a long knife. His zarape, of Indian fabric and showy colours, was folded on the back of his horse, an animal full of fire, with fine legs, small head, and flashing eye. It was a true prairie mustang; and its master had decorated it with the coquettish elegance peculiar to Mexican horsemen.

In addition to the knife we referred to, and which the horseman wore in his right boot, he had also a long American rifle laid across his saddle-bow, two six-shot revolvers in his girdle, a *machete*, or species of straight sabre, which was passed, unsheathed, through an iron ring on his left side; and, lastly, a *reata* of plaited leather, rolled up and fastened to the saddle.

Thus armed, the man we have just described was able—on the admission that his determined appearance was not deceitful—to make head against several adversaries at once, without any serious disadvantage. This was a consideration not at all to be despised in a country where a traveller ever runs the risk of encountering an enemy, whether man or beast, and, at times, both together.

While galloping, the horseman carelessly smoked a husk cigarette, only taking an absent and disdainful glance at the coveys of birds that rose on his approach, or the herds of deer and packs of foxes which fled in terror on hearing the horse's gallop.

The savannah, however, was already beginning to assume a more gloomy tinge; the sun, now level with the ground, only appeared on the horizon as a red unheated ball, and night was soon about to cover the earth with its dense gloom. The horseman drew up the bridle of his steed to check its speed, though not entirely stopping it, and, casting an investigating glance around him, seemed to be seeking a suitable spot for his night halt.

After a few seconds of this search, the traveller's determination was formed. He turned slightly to the left, and proceeded to a half-dried-up stream that ran along a short distance off, and on whose banks grew a few prickly shrubs and a clump of some dozen larches, forming a precarious shelter against the curiosity of those mysterious denizens of the desert that prowl about in search of prey during the darkness.

On drawing nearer, the traveller perceived to his delight that this spot, perfectly hidden from prying glances, by the conformation of the ground and a few blocks of stone scattered here and there among the trees and shrubs, offered him an almost certain shelter.

The journey had been tiring; and both man and horse felt themselves worn with fatigue. Both, before proceeding further, imperiously required a few hours' rest.

The horseman, as an experienced traveller, first attended to his steed, which he unsaddled and led to drink at the stream; then, after hobbling the animal for fear it might stray and become the prey of wild beasts, he stretched his zarape on the ground, threw a few handfuls of Indian corn upon it, and when he was assured that his horse, in spite of its fatigue, was eating its provender willingly, he thought about himself.

Mexicans, when travelling, carry behind their saddle two canvas bags, called *alforjas*, intended to convey food, which it is impossible to procure in the desert; and these, with two jars filled with drinking water, form the sole baggage with which they cover enormous distances, and endure privations and fatigue, the mere enumeration of which would terrify Europeans, who are accustomed to enjoy all the conveniences supplied by an advanced stage of civilization.

The horseman opened his alforjas, sat down on the ground with his back against a rock, and, while careful that his weapons were within reach, for fear of being attacked unawares, he began supping philosophically on a piece of tasajo, some maize tortillas, and goat's cheese as hard as a flint, the whole being washed down with the pure water of the stream.

This repast, which was more than frugal, was soon terminated. The horseman, after cleaning his teeth with an elegant gold toothpick, rolled a pajillo, smoked it with that conscientious beatitude peculiar to the Hispano-Americans, and then wrapped himself in his zarape, shut his eyes, and fell asleep.

Several hours passed; and it is probable that the traveller's sleep would have been prolonged for some time, had not two shots, fired a short distance from him, suddenly aroused him from his lethargy. The general rule on the prairie is, that when you hear a shot, it is rare for it not to have been preceded by the whistle of a bullet past your ear—in other words, there are ninety-nine reasons in a hundred that the lonely man has been unconsciously converted into the target of an assassin.

The traveller, thus unpleasantly aroused, seized his weapons, concealed himself behind a rock, and waited. Then, as after the expiration of a moment the attack was not renewed, he rose softly, and carefully looked around him.

Not a sound disturbed the majestic solitude of the desert. But this sudden tranquillity after the two shots, instead of reassuring the traveller, only augmented his anxiety, by revealing to him the approach of a certain danger, though it was impossible for him to divine the cause or the magnitude.

The night was clear, and, so to speak, transparent; the sky, of a deep blue, was studded with a profusion of sparkling stars, and the moon shed a white and melancholy light, that allowed the country to be surveyed for a long distance.

At all hazards he saddled his horse; then, after concealing it in a rocky cavity, he lay down, placed his ear to the ground, and listened. Then he fancied he could hear a long distance off a sound, at first almost imperceptible, but which rapidly approached; and he soon recognised in it the wild galloping of several horses.

It was a hunt, or a pursuit. But who would dream of hunting in the middle of the night? The Indians would not venture it, while white and half-bred trappers only rarely visited these deserted regions, which they abandoned to the savages and border-ruffians; utter villains, who, expelled from the towns and pueblos, have no other shelter than the desert.

Were the galloping horsemen pirates of the prairie, then?

The situation was becoming painful to

the traveller, when, all at once, the noise ceased, and all became silent.

The traveller rose from the ground.

Suddenly, the shrieks of a woman or girl burst forth on the night, with an expression of terror and agony impossible to depict.

The stranger, leaving his horse in the shelter he had selected for it, dashed forward in the direction whence the cry came, leaping from rock to rock and clearing shrubs, at the risk of hurting himself, with the feverish speed of the brave man who believes himself suddenly called by Providence to save a fellow-being in danger.

Still, prudence did not desert him in his hazardous enterprise; and, before risking himself on the plain, he stopped behind a fringe of larch-trees, in order to try and find out what was going on, and act in accordance.

This is what he saw:—Two men, who from their appearance he at once recognised as belonging to the worst species of prairie-runners, were madly pursuing a young girl. But, thanks to her juvenile agility—an agility doubtless doubled by the profound terror the bandits inspired her with—this maiden bounded like a startled fawn across the prairie, leaping ravines, clearing every obstacle, and gaining at each moment a greater advance on her pursuers, who were impeded by their vaquera boots and heavy rifles.

A few minutes later, and the maiden reached the belt of trees behind which the traveller had concealed himself. The latter was about to rush to her assistance, when suddenly one of the bandits raised his rifle and pulled the trigger.

The girl fell, and the horseman seemed to change his mind—for, instead of advancing, he drew himself back and stood motionless, with his finger on the trigger, and ready to fire.

The pirates rapidly approached, talking together in that medley of English, French, Spanish, and Indian which is employed throughout the Far West.

"Hum!" said a hoarse and panting voice; "what a gazelle! At one moment I really thought she would escape us."

"Yes, yes," the other answered, shaking his head and tapping the barrel of his rifle with his right hand; "but I always felt certain of bringing her down when I thought proper."

"Yes, and you did not miss her, *caraï!* although it was a long shot, and your hand must have trembled after such a chase."

"Habit, compadre! habit!" the bandit answered, with a modest smile.

While talking thus, the two bandits had reached the spot where the body of the girl lay. One of them knelt down, doubtless to assure himself of the death of their victim; while the other, the one who had fired, looked on carelessly, leaning on his rifle.

The traveller then drew himself up, raised his piece, and fired. The bandit, struck in the centre of the breast, sank down like a sack, and did not stir. He was dead.

His companion had started and laid his hand on his *machete;* but not leaving him time to employ it, the traveller rushed on him, and with a powerful blow of the butt-end on his head, sent him to join his comrade on the ground, where he rolled, half killed.

The traveller, taking the bandit's *reata,* then firmly bound his hands and feet; and, easy in mind on this point, he eagerly approached the maiden. The poor girl gave no sign of life, but, for all that, was not dead; her wound, indeed, was slight, as the pirate's bullet had merely grazed her arm. Terror alone had produced her fainting fit.

The stranger carefully bandaged the wound, slightly moistened her lips and temples, and, after a comparatively short period, had the satisfaction of seeing her open her eyes again.

"Oh!" she murmured, in a voice soft and melodious as a bird's song, "those men—those demons! Oh! Heaven! protect me!"

"Reassure yourself, Senorita," the traveller answered; "you have nothing further to fear from those villains."

The maiden started at the sound of this strange voice; she fixed her eyes on the stranger without giving him any answer, and made an instinctive movement to rise. She doubtless took the man who had spoken to her for one of her pursuers. The latter smiled mournfully, and pointed to the two bandits lying on the ground.

"Look, Senorita," he said to her; "you have only a friend here."

At this sight an expression of unbounded gratitude illumined the wounded girl's face, and a sickly smile appeared on her lips; but almost immediately her features grew saddened again. She sprang up, and raising herself on the tips of her small feet, she stretched out her right arm toward a point on the horizon, and exclaimed in a voice broken by terror—

"There, there! Look!"

The stranger turned to the indicated direction. A party of horsemen were coming up at full speed, preceded about a rifle-shot distance by another horseman, evidently better mounted than they, and whom they appeared to be pursuing. The stranger then remembered the furious galloping he had heard a few moments previously.

"Oh!" the girl exclaimed, clasping her hands in entreaty, "save him, Senor! Save him!"

"I will try, Senorita," he replied, gently; "all that a man can do I swear to do."

"Thank you," she said, offering him her pretty little hand; "you are a noble-hearted man, and Heaven will aid you."

"You must not remain here exposed to the insults of these men, who are evidently the comrades of those from whom you have just escaped."

"That is true," she said; "but what can I do? Where shall I seek shelter?"

"Follow me behind these trees; we have not a moment to lose."

"Come," she said, resolutely. "But you will save him! Will you not?"

"At least I will try. I have only my life to offer the person in whom you take an interest; and believe me, Senorita, I shall not hesitate to make the sacrifice."

The maiden looked down with a blush, and silently followed her guide. They soon reached the thicket in which the stranger had established his quarters for the night.

"Whatever happens," he said, while reloading his rifle, "remain here, Senorita. You are in safety in this hollow rock, where no one will dream of seeking you. For my part, I am going to help your friend."

"Go," she said, as she knelt down on the ground; "while you are fighting I will pray for you—and Heaven will grant my prayer."

"Yes," the stranger answered, mournfully, "God listens gladly to the voice of angels, so let us hope for the best."

He leaped on his horse; and after giving a parting glance at the maiden, who was praying fervently, he dashed at full speed in the direction of the new comers. There were seven in number—bandits with stern faces and dangerous aspect, who dashed up brandishing their weapons and uttering horrible yells.

The pursued horseman, on seeing a man emerge so unexpectedly from the thicket, and come towards him at full speed, rifle in hand, naturally supposed that assistance was arriving for his foes, and dashed on one side to avoid a man whom he assumed, with some show of reason, to be an adversary the more. But the bandits were not mistaken when they saw the stranger not only let their prey escape, but stop in front of them and cock his rifle.

Two shots were fired at the same moment, one by a bandit, the other by the stranger, with the difference, however, that the bandit's shot, being fired haphazard, was harmless; while the stranger's, being deliberately aimed, struck exactly in the mass of his serried foes.

A few seconds later, one of them let go his bridle, beat the air with his arms, fell back on his horse, and at length on the ground, tearing with his huge spurs the sides of his steed, which reared, kicked, and started off like an arrow.

A war so frankly declared could not have

a sudden termination: four shots succeeding each other with extreme rapidity on either side were a sufficient proof of this. But the stranger's position was growing critical: his rifle was discharged, and he had only his revolvers left.

The revolver, by the way, is a weapon more convenient than useful in a fight, for if you wish to hit your man, you must fire at him almost point blank, otherwise the bullets have a tendency to stray. This is a sufficient explanation why, in spite of the immoderate use the North Americans make of this weapon, the number of murders among them is proportionately limited.

The stranger was, therefore, somewhat embarrassed, and was preparing in his emergency for a hand-to-hand fight, when help he had been far from calculating on suddenly reached him.

The pursued horseman, on hearing the firing, and yet finding that no bullets whizzed past him, understood that something unusual was taking place, and that some strange incident must have occurred in his favour. Hence he turned back, and saw one of his enemies fall. Recognising his mistake, he made up his mind at once: though only armed with a *machete*, he wheeled his horse round and bravely drew up alongside his defender.

Then the two men, without exchanging a word, resolutely dashed at the bandits. The contest was short—the success unhoped for. Moreover, the sides were nearly equal, for of the seven pirates only four were now alive.

The attack was so sudden, that the pirates had not time to reload. Two were killed with revolver-shots. The third fell with his head severed by a *machete* blow from the horseman, who was burning to take an exemplary vengeance; while the fourth, finding himself alone, leaped his horse over the corpses of his comrades, and fled at full speed without attempting to continue longer a combat which could not but be fatal to him.

The two men consequently remained masters of the battle-field.

CHAPTER II.

ON THE PRAIRIE.

When the last bandit had disappeared in the darkness, the horseman turned to his generous defender, in order to thank him; but the latter was no longer by his side, and he saw him galloping some distance off on the plain.

The horseman knew not to what he should attribute this sudden departure—(for the stranger was following a direction diametrically opposite to that on which the pirate had fled)—till he saw him return, leading another horse by the bridle.

The stranger had thought of the young lady he had so miraculously saved; and on seeing the horses of the killed bandits galloping about, he resolved at once to capture the best of them, in order to enable her to continue her journey more comfortably; and when the animal was lassoed, he returned slowly towards the man to whom he had rendered so great a service.

"Senor," the horseman said, as soon as they met again, "all is not over yet; I have a further service to ask of you."

"Speak, Caballero," the stranger replied, starting at the sound of the voice, which he fancied he recognised. "Speak, I am listening to you."

"A woman, an unhappy girl—my sister, in a word, is lost in this horrible desert. Some of the scoundrels started in pursuit of her, and I know not what may have happened to her. I am in mortal agony, and must rejoin her at all risks; hence do not leave the good action you have so well begun unfinished; help me to find my sister's track, —join with me in seeking her."

"It is useless," the stranger answered, coldly.

"What, useless!" the horseman exclaimed with horror; "has any misfortune happened to her? Ah! I remember now; I fancied, while I was flying, that I heard several shots. Oh, Heaven, Heaven!" he added, writhing his hands in despair, "my poor sister, my poor Marianita!"

"Reassure yourself, Caballero," the stranger continued in the same cold deliberate accent; "your sister is in safety, temporarily at least, and has nothing to fear. Heaven permitted that I should cross her path."

"Are you stating truth?" he exclaimed, joyfully. "Oh, bless you, Senor, for the happy news! Where is she? Let me see her! Let me press her to my heart! Alas! how shall I ever acquit my debt to you?"

"You owe me nothing," the stranger answered in a rough voice; "it was chance, or God, if you prefer it, that did everything, and I was only the instrument. My conduct would have been the same to any other person; so keep your gratitude—which I do not ask of you. Who knows," he added, ironically, "whether you may not some day repent of having contracted any obligations toward me?"

The horseman felt internally pained at the way in which his advances were received by a man who scarce five minutes previously had saved his life. Not knowing to what he should attribute this sudden change of temper, he pretended not to notice anything offensive the words might contain, and said, with exquisite politeness—

"The spot is badly chosen for a lengthened conversation, Caballero. We are still, if not strangers, at least unknown to each other. I trust that ere long all coldness and misunderstanding will cease between us, and make room for perfect confidence."

The other smiled bitterly.

"Come," he said, "your sister is near here, and must be impatient to see you."

The horseman followed him without replying; but asking himself mentally who this singular man could be, who risked his life to defend him, and yet appeared anxious to treat him as an enemy.

All the sounds of the combat had reached the maiden's ear: she had heard them while kneeling on the ground, half dead with terror, and searching her troubled memory in vain for a prayer to address to Heaven.

Then the firing had ceased: a mournful silence again spread over the desert—a silence more terrifying a thousand-fold than the terrible sounds of the fight, and she remained crouching in a corner and suffering from nameless agony, alone, far from all human help, not daring to retain a single hope, and fearing at each moment to see a frightful death awaiting her.

The poor girl could not have said how long she remained thus crushed beneath the weight of her terror. A person must really have suffered, to know of how many centuries a minute is composed when life or death is awaited.

Suddenly she started: her strong nerves relaxed, a fugitive flush tinged her cheek, she fancied she had heard a few words uttered in a low voice not far from her. Were her enemies again pursuing her? or was her saviour returning to her side?

She remained anxious and motionless, not daring to make a movement or utter a cry to ask for help; for a movement might reveal her presence, a cry hopelessly ruin her.

But, ere long, the bushes were parted by a powerful hand: and two horsemen appeared at the base of the rock. The maiden stretched out her hands to them with an exclamation of delight; and, too weak to support this last emotion, she fainted.

She had recognised in the men, who arrived side by side, her brother and the stranger to whom she owed her life.

When she regained her senses, she was lying on furs in front of a large fire. The two men were sitting on her right and left; while in the rock-cave, three horses were eating their provender of alfalfa.

Somewhat in the shadow, a few paces from her, the maiden perceived a mass, whose form it was impossible for her to distinguish at the first glance, but which a more attentive examination enabled her to recognise as a bound man lying on the ground.

The maiden was anxious to speak and thank her liberator; but the shock she had received was so rude, the emotion so powerful, that it was impossible for her to utter a word—so weak did she feel. She could only give him a glance full of all the gratitude she felt, and then fell back into a species of feverish exhaustion and morbid apathy, which almost completely deprived her of the power of thinking and feeling, and which rendered her involuntarily ignorant of all that was going on around her.

"It is well," said the stranger, as he carefully closed a gold-mounted flask and concealed it in his bosom. "Now, Caballero, there is nothing more to fear for the

Senorita; the draught I have administered to her, by procuring her a calm and healthy sleep, will restore her strength sufficiently for her to be able to continue her journey at sunrise, should it be necessary."

"Caballero," the stranger answered, "you are really performing the part of Providence towards me and my sister. I know not, in truth, how to express to you the lively gratitude I feel for a procedure which is the more generous as I am a perfect stranger to you."

"Do you think so?" he answered sarcastically.

"The more I examine your face, the more convinced I am that I have met you to-night for the first time."

"You would not venture to affirm it?"

"Yes, I would. Your features are too remarkable for me not to remember them if I had seen you before; but I repeat, if you fancy you know me, you are mistaken, and an accidental resemblance to some other person is the cause of your error."

There was a momentary silence, and then the stranger spoke again, with a politeness too affected for the irony it concealed not to be seen—

"Be it so, Caballero," he answered, with a bow; "perhaps I am mistaken. Be good enough, therefore, if you have no objection, to tell me who you are, and by what fortuitous concourse of circumstances I have been enabled to render you what you are kind enough to call a great service?"

"And it is an immense one, in truth, Caballero," the stranger interrupted, with warmth.

"I will not discuss that subject any longer with you, Caballero; I am awaiting your pleasure."

"Senor, I will not abuse your patience for long. My name is Don Ruiz de Moguer, and I reside with my father at a hacienda in the vicinity of Arispe. For reasons too lengthy to explain to you, and which would but slightly interest you, the presence of my sister (who has been at school for some years at the Convent of the Conception at El Rosario) became indispensable at the hacienda. By my father's orders I set out for El Rosario a few months ago, in order to bring my sister back to her family. I was anxious to rejoin my father; and hence, in spite of the observations made to me by persons acquainted with the dangers attending so long a journey through a desert country, I resolved to take no escort, but start for home merely accompanied by two peons, on whose courage and fidelity I could rely.

"My sister, who had been separated from her family for several years, was as eager as myself to quit the convent; and hence we soon set out. For the first few days all went well; our journey was performed under the most favourable auspices, and my sister and I laughed at the anxiety and apprehensions of our friends, for we had begun to believe ourselves safe from any dangerous encounter.

"But yesterday, at sunset, just as we were preparing our camp for the night, we were suddenly attacked by a party of bandits, who seemed to emerge from the ground in front of us, so unforeseen was their apparition. Our poor brave peons were killed while defending us; and my sister's horse, struck by a bullet in the head, threw her. But the brave girl, far from surrendering to the bandits, who rushed forward to seize her, began flying across the savannah. Then I tried to lead the aggressors off the scent, and induce them to pursue me. You know the rest, Caballero; and had it not been for your providential interference, it would have been all over with us."

There was a silence, which Don Ruiz was the first to break.

"Caballero," he said, "now that you know who I am, tell me the name of my saviour?"

"What good is that?" the stranger answered, sadly. "We have come together for a moment by chance, and shall separate to-morrow never to meet again. Gratitude is a heavy burden. Not knowing who I am, you will soon have forgotten me. Believe me, Senor Don Ruiz, it is better that it should be so. Who knows if you may not regret some day knowing me?"

"It is the second time you have said that, Caballero. Your words breathe a bitterness that pains me. You must have suffered very grievously for your thoughts to be so sad and your heart so disenchanted at an age when the future ordinarily appears so full of promise."

The stranger raised his head, and bent on his questioner a glance that seemed trying to read to the bottom of his soul: the latter continued, however, with some degree of vivacity—

"Oh! do not mistake the meaning I attach to my words, Caballero. I have no intention to take your confidence by surprise, or encroach on your secrets. Every man's life belongs to himself—his actions concern himself alone; and I recognise no claim to a confidence which I neither expect nor desire. The only thing I ask of you is to tell me your name, that my sister and myself may retain it in our hearts."

"Why insist on so frivolous a matter?"

"I will answer—What reason have you to be so obstinate in remaining unknown?"

"Then you insist on my telling you my name?"

"Oh, Caballero, I have no right to insist; I only ask it."

"Very good," said the stranger, "you shall know my name; but I warn you that it will teach you nothing."

"Pardon me, Caballero," Don Ruiz remarked, with a touch of exquisite delicacy, "this name, repeated by me to my father, will tell him every hour in the day that it is to the man who bears it that he owes the life of his children, and a whole family will bless you."

In spite of himself, the stranger felt affected. By an instinctive movement he offered his hand to the young man, which the latter pressed affectionately. But, as if suddenly reproaching himself for yielding to his feelings, this strange man sharply drew back his hand, and reassuming the expression of sternness, which had for a moment departed from him, said, with a roughness in his voice that astonished and saddened the young Mexican,

"You shall be satisfied."

We have said that Dona Marianita, in looking round her, fancied she saw the body of a man stretched on the ground a few paces from the fire. The maiden was not mistaken; it was really a man she saw, carefully gagged and bound. It was, in a word, one of the two bandits who had pursued her so long, and the one whom the stranger had almost killed with a blow of his rifle-butt.

After recommending Don Ruiz to be patient by a wave of his hand, the stranger rose, walked straight up to the bandit, threw him on his shoulders, and laid him at the feet of the young Mexican, perhaps rather roughly—for the pirate, in spite of the thorough Indian stoicism he affected, could not suppress a stifled yell of pain.

"Who is this man, and what do you purpose doing with him?" Don Ruiz asked, with some anxiety.

"This scoundrel," the stranger answered, harshly, "was one of the band that attacked you; we are going to try him."

"Try him?" the young gentleman objected; "we?"

"Of course," the stranger said, as he removed the bandit's gag, and unfastened the rope that bound his limbs. "Do you fancy that we are going to trouble ourselves with the scoundrel till we find a prison in which to place him, without counting the fact that, if we were so simple as to do so, the odds are about fifty to one that he would escape from us during the journey, and slip through our fingers like an opossum, to attack us a few hours later at the head of a fresh band of pirates of his own breed. No, no; that would be madness. When the snake is dead, the venom is dead, too; it is better to try him."

"But by what right can we constitute ourselves the judges of this man?"

"By what right?" the stranger exclaimed, in amazement. "The Border law, which says, 'Eye for eye; tooth for tooth.' Lynch law authorizes us to try this bandit, and when the sentence is pronounced, to execute it ourselves."

Don Ruiz reflected for a moment, during which the stranger looked at him aside with the most serious attention.

"That is possible," the young man at length answered; "perhaps you are right in speaking thus. This man is guilty—he is evidently a miserable assassin covered with blood; and, had my sister and myself fallen into his hands, he would not have hesitated to stab us, or blow out our brains."

"Well?" the stranger remarked.

"Well," the young man continued, with generous animation in his voice; "this certainly does not authorize us in taking justice into our own hands; besides, my sister is saved."

"Then, it is your opinion ——"

"That, as we cannot hand this man over to the police, we are bound to set him at liberty, after taking all proper precautions that he cannot injure us."

"You have, doubtless, carefully reflected

on the consequences of the deed you advise?"

"My conscience orders me to act as I am doing."

"Your will be done!" and, addressing the bandit, who throughout the conversation had remained gloomy and silent, though his eyes constantly wandered from one to the other of the speakers, he said to him, "Get up!"

The pirate rose.

"Look at me," the stranger continued; "do you recognise me?"

"No," the bandit said.

The stranger seized a lighted brand, and held it up near his face.

"Look at me more carefully, Kidd," he said, in a sharp, imperious voice.

The scoundrel, who had bent forward, drew himself back with a start of fear.

"Stronghand!" he exclaimed, in a voice choked by dread.

"Ah!" the horseman said, with a sardonic smile; "I see that you recognise me now."

"Yes," the bandit muttered. "What are your orders?"

"I have none. You heard all we have been saying, I suppose?"

"All."

"What do you think of it?"

The pirate did not answer.

"Speak, and be frank! I insist."

"Hum!" he said, with a side glance.

"Will you speak? I tell you I insist."

"Well!" he answered, in a rather humbling voice, but yet with a tinge of irony easy to notice; "I think that when you hold your enemy, you ought to kill him."

"That is really your opinion?"

"Yes."

"What do you say to that?" the stranger asked, turning to Don Ruiz.

"I say," he replied, simply, "that as this man is not my enemy, I cannot and ought not to take any vengeance on him."

"Hence?"

"Hence, justice alone has the right to make him account for his conduct. As for me, I decline."

"And that is truly the expression of your thoughts?"

"On my honour, Caballero. During the fight I should not have felt the slightest hesitation in killing him—for in that case I was defending the life he tried to take; but now that he is a prisoner, and unarmed, I have no longer aught to do with him."

In spite of the mask of indifference the stranger wore on his face, he could not completely hide the joy he experienced at hearing these noble sentiments so simply expressed.

There was a moment's silence, during which the three men seemed questioning each other's faces. At length Stronghand spoke again, and addressed the bandit, who remained motionless, and apparently indifferent to what was being said—

"Go! you are free!" he said, as he cut the last bonds that held him. "But remember, Kidd, that if it has pleased this Caballero to forget your offences, I have not pardoned them. You know me, so do your best to keep out of my way, or you will not escape, so easily as this day, the just punishment you have deserved. Begone!"

"All right, Stronghand, I will remember," the bandit said, with a covert threat.

And at once gliding into the bushes, he disappeared, without taking further leave of the persons who had given him his life.

CHAPTER III.

THE BIVOUAC.

For some moments the bandit's hurried footsteps were audible, and then all became silent once again.

"You wished it," Stronghand then said, looking at Don Ruiz from under his bent brows. "Now, be certain that you have at least one implacable enemy on the prairie; for you are not so simple, I assume, as to believe in the gratitude of such a man?"

"I pity him, if he hates me for the good I have done him in return for the harm he wished to do me, but honour ordered me to let him escape."

"Yours will be a short life, Senor, if you are obstinate in carrying out such philanthropic precepts in our unhappy country."

"My ancestors had a motto to which they never proved false."

"And pray what may that motto be, Caballero?"

"'Everything for honour, no matter what may happen,'" the young man said, simply.

"Yes," Stronghand answered, with a harsh laugh; "the maxim is noble, and Heaven grant it prove of service to you; but," he continued, after looking round him, "the darkness is beginning to grow less thick, the night is on the wane, and within an hour the sun will be up. You know my name, which, as I told you beforehand, has not helped you much."

"You are mistaken, Caballero," Don Ruiz interrupted him, eagerly; "for I have frequently heard the name mentioned, of which you fancied me ignorant."

Stronghand bent a piercing glance on the young man.

"Ah!" he said, with a slight tremor in his voice; "and doubtless, each time you heard that name uttered, it was accompanied by far from flattering epithets, which gave you but a poor opinion of the man who bears it."

"Here again you are mistaken, Senor; it has been uttered in my presence as the name of a brave man, with a powerful heart and vast intellect, whom unknown and secret sorrow has urged to lead a strange life, to fly the society of his fellow-men, and to wander constantly about the deserts; but who, under all circumstances, even spite of the examples that daily surrounded him, managed to keep his honour intact and retain a spotless reputation, which even the bandits, with whom the incidents of an adventurous life too often bring him into contact, are forced to admire. That, Senor, is what this name, which you supposed I was ignorant of, recals to my mind, and the way in which I have ever heard the man who bears it spoken of."

Stronghand smiled bitterly.

"Can the world really be less wicked and unjust than I supposed it?" he muttered, in self-colloquy.

"Do not doubt it," the young man said, eagerly. "God, who has allowed the good and the bad to dwell side by side on this earth, has yet willed that the amount of good should exceed that of bad, so that, sooner or later, each should be requited according to his works and merits."

"Such words," he answered, ironically,

"would be more appropriate in the mouth of a priest or missionary, whose hair has been blanched, and back bowed by the weight of the incessant struggles of his apostolic mission, than in that of a young man who has scarce reached the dawn of life, whom no tempest has yet assailed, and who has only tasted the honey of life. But no matter; your intention is good, and I thank you. But we have far more serious matters to attend to than losing our time in philosophical discussions which would not convince either of us."

"I was wrong, Caballero, I allow," Don Ruiz answered; "it does not become me, who am as yet but a child, to make such remarks to you; so, pray pardon me."

"I have nothing to pardon you, Senor," Stronghand replied with a smile; "on the contrary, I thank you. Now let us attend to the most pressing affair—that is to say, what you purpose doing to get out of your present situation."

"I confess to you that I am greatly alarmed," Don Ruiz replied, with a slight tinge of sadness, as he looked at the girl, who was still sleeping. "What has happened to me, the terrible danger I have incurred, and from which I only escaped, thanks to your generous help——"

"Not a word more on that subject," Stronghand interrupted him quickly. "You will disoblige me by pressing it further."

The young man bowed.

"Were I alone," he said, "I should not hesitate to continue my journey. A brave man, and I believe myself one, nearly always succeeds in escaping the perils that threaten him, if he confront them: but I have my sister with me—my sister, whose energy the terrible scene of this night has broken, and who, in the event of a second attack from the pirates of the prairies, would become an easy prey to the villains—the more so because, too weak to save her, I could only die with her."

Stronghand turned away, murmuring to himself compassionately,

"That is true, poor child;" then he said to Don Ruiz, "Still, you must make up your mind."

"Unfortunately I have no choice; there is only one thing to be done: whatever may happen, I shall continue my journey at sunrise, if my sister be in a condition to follow me."

"That need not trouble you. When she awakes, her strength will be sufficiently recovered for her to keep on horseback without excessive fatigue; but from here to Arispe the road is very long."

"I know it; and it is that which frightens me for my poor sister."

"Listen to me. Perhaps there is a way for you to get out of the scrape, and avoid up to a certain point the dangers that threaten you. Two days' journey from here there is a military post, placed like an advanced sentry to watch the frontier, and prevent the incursions of the Indios bravos, and other bandits of every description and colour, who infest these regions. The main point for you is to reach this post, when it will be easy for you to obtain from the Commandant an escort to protect you from any insult for the rest of your journey."

"Yes; but, as you remark, I must reach the post."

"Well?"

"I do not know this country: one of the two peons who accompanied me acted as guide; and now he is dead it is utterly impossible for me to find my way. I am in the position of a sailor, lost without a compass on an unknown sea."

Stronghand looked at him with surprise mingled with compassion.

"Oh!" he exclaimed, "how improvident is youth! What! imprudent boy! you dared to risk yourself in the desert, and entrust to a peon your sister's precious life?" But, recollecting himself immediately, he continued, "Pardon me; reproaches are ill-suited at this moment; the great thing is to get you out of the danger in which you are."

He let his head fall on his hands, and plunged into serious reflections, while Don Ruiz looked at him with mingled apprehension and hope. The young man did not deceive himself as to his position: the reproaches which Stronghand spared him he had already made himself, cursing his improvident temerity; for things had reached such a point, that if the man to whom he already owed his life refused to afford him his omnipotent protection, he and his sister were irremediably lost.

Stronghand, after a few minutes, which

seemed to the young man to last an age, rose, seized his rifle, went up to his horse, saddled it, mounted, and said to Don Ruiz, who followed all his movements with anxious curiosity—

"Wait for me, however long my absence may be; do not stir from here till I return."

Then, without waiting for the young man's answer, he bent lightly over his horse's neck, and started at a gallop. Don Ruiz watched the black outline, as it disappeared in the gloom; he listened to the horse's foot-falls so long as he could hear them, and then turned back and seated himself pensively at the fire, and looked with tearful eyes at his sleeping sister.

"Poor Marianita!" he murmured, with a heart-rending outburst of pity.

He bowed his head on his chest, and with pale and gloomy face awaited the return of Stronghand—a return which, in his heart, he doubted, although, with the obstinacy of desperate men, who try to deceive themselves by making excuses whose falsehood they know, he sought to prove its certainty.

We will take advantage of this delay in one narrative to trace rapidly the portraits of Don Ruiz de Moguer and his sister Marianita. We will begin with the young lady, through politeness.

Dona Mariana—or rather Marianita, as she was generally called at the convent and by her family—was a charming girl scarce sixteen, graceful in her movements, and with black lustrous eyes. Her hair had the bluish tinge of the raven's wing; her skin, the warm and gilded hues of the sun of her country; her glance, half veiled by her long brown eyelashes, was ardent; her straight nose, with its pink flexible nostrils, was delicious; her laughing mouth, with its bright red lips, gave her face an expression of simple, ignorant candour. Her movements, soft and indolent, had that indescribable languor and serpentine undulation alone possessed in so eminent a degree by the women of Lima and Mexico, those daughters of the sun in whose veins flows the molten lava of their volcanoes, instead of blood. In a word, she was a Spanish girl from head to foot—but Andalusian before all. Hers was an ardent, wild, jealous, passionate, and excessively superstitious nature. But this lovely, splendid statue still wanted the divine spark. Dona Mariana did not know herself; her heart had not yet spoken; she was as yet but a delicious child, whom the fiery breath of love would convert into an adorable woman.

Physically, Don Ruiz was, as a man, the same his sister was as a woman. He was a thorough gentleman, and scarce four years older than Dona Mariana. He was tall and well-built; but his elegant and aristocratic form denoted great personal strength. His regular features—too regular, perhaps, for a man—bore an unmistakeable stamp of distinction; his black eye had a frank and confident look; his mouth, which was rather large, but adorned with splendid teeth and fringed by a fine brown moustache coquettishly turned up, still retained the joyous, careless smile of youth; his face displayed loyalty, gentleness, and bravery carried to temerity;—in a word, all his features offered the most perfect type of a true-blooded gentleman.

Brother and sister, who, with the exception of a few almost imperceptible variations, had the most perfect physical likeness, also resembled each other morally. Both were equally ignorant of things of the world. With their pure and innocent hearts they loved each other with the holiest of all loves, fraternal affection, and only lived through and for each other.

Hence, Dona Mariana had felt a great delight and great impatience to quit the convent, when Don Ruiz, in obedience to his father's commands, came to fetch her from the Rosario. This impatience obliged Don Ruiz not to consent to wait for an escort on his homeward journey, for fear of vexing his sister. It was an imprudence that caused the misfortunes we have already described, and for which, now they had arrived, Don Ruiz reproached himself bitterly. He cursed the weakness that had made him yield to the whims of a girl, and accused himself of being, through his weakness, the sole cause of the frightful dangers from which she had only escaped by a miracle, and of those no less terrible, which, doubtless, still threatened her on the hundred and odd leagues they had still to go before reaching the hacienda del Toro, where dwelt her father, Don Hernando de Moguer.

Still the hours, which never stop, continued to follow each other slowly. The sun had risen; and, through its presence on the horizon, immediately dissipated the darkness and heated the ground, which was chilled by the abundant and icy dew of morning.

Dona Marianita, aroused by the singing of the thousands of birds concealed beneath the foliage, opened her eyes with a smile. The calm sleep she had enjoyed for several hours restored not only her strength, which was exhausted by the struggles of the previous evening, but also her courage and gaiety. The girl's first glance was for her brother, who, anxious and uneasy, was attentively watching her slumbers, and impatiently awaiting the moment for her to awake.

"Oh, Ruiz," she said, in her melodious voice, and offering her hand and cheek simultaneously to the young man, "what a glorious sleep I have had."

"Really, sister," he exclaimed, kissing her, gladly, "you have slept well."

"That is to say," she continued, with a smile, "that at the convent I never passed so delicious a night, accompanied by such charming dreams; but it is true there were two of you to watch over my slumbers—two kind and devoted hearts, in whom I could trust with perfect confidence."

"Yes, sister; there were two of us."

"What?" she asked, with a surprise mingled with anxiety. "You were—— What do you mean, Ruiz?"

"What I say; nothing else, dear sister."

"But I do not see the caballero to whom we have incurred so great an obligation. Where is he?"

"I cannot tell you, little sister. About two hours ago he mounted his horse and left me, telling me not to stir from here till his return."

"Oh, in that case I am quite easy. His absence alarmed me; but now that I know he will return——"

"Do you believe so?" he interrupted.

"Why should I doubt it?" she continued, with some animation in her voice; "did he not promise to return?"

"Certainly."

"Well! a caballero never breaks his pledged word. He said he would come, and he will come."

"Heaven grant it!" Don Ruiz muttered.

And he shook his head sadly, and gave a profound sigh. The maiden felt herself involuntarily assailed by anxiety. This persistency undoubtedly terrified her.

"Come, Ruiz," she said, turning very pale, "explain yourself. What has happened between this caballero and yourself?"

"Nothing beyond what you know, sister. Still, in spite of the man's promise, I know not why, but I fear. He is a strange, incomprehensible being—at one moment kind, at another cruel—changing his character, and almost his face, momentarily. He frightens and repels, and yet attracts and interests me. I am afraid he will abandon us, and fear that he will return. A secret foreboding seems to warn me that this man will have a great influence over your future and mine. Perhaps it is for our misfortune that we have met him."

"I do not understand you, Ruiz. What means this confusion in your ideas? Why this stern and strange judgment of a man whom you do not know, and who has only done you kindness?"

At the moment when Don Ruiz was preparing to answer, the gallop of a horse became audible in the distance.

"Silence, brother!" she exclaimed, with an emotion she could not repress; "silence, here he comes!"

The young man looked at his sister in amazement.

"How do you know it?" he asked her.

"I have recognised him," she stammered, with a deep blush. "Stay—Look!"

In fact, at this moment the shrubs parted, and Stronghand appeared in the open space. Don Ruiz, though surprised at the singular remark which had escaped his sister, had not the time to ask her for an explanation. Without dismounting, Stronghand, after bowing courteously to the young lady, said, hurriedly—

"To horse!—to horse! Make haste! Time presses!"

Don Ruiz at once saddled his own horse and his sister's, and a few minutes later the two young people were riding by the hunter's side.

"Let us start!" the latter continued. "*Cuerpo de Cristo*, Caballero, I warned you that you were doing an imprudent action in liberating that villain. If we do not take care, we shall have him at our heels within an hour."

These words sufficed to give the fugitives wings, and they started at full gallop after the bold woodranger. An hour elapsed ere a word was exchanged between the three persons; bent over the necks of their steeds they devoured the space—looking back anxiously from time to time, and only thinking how to escape the unknown dangers by which they felt themselves surrounded. About eight o'clock in the morning, Stronghand checked his horse, and made his companions a sign to follow his example.

"Now," he said, "we have nothing more to fear. When we have crossed that wood, which stretches out in front of us like a curtain of verdure, we shall see the Fort of San Miguel, whose walls will offer us a certain shelter against the attacks of all the bandits of the desert, were there ten thousand of them."

"Last night I fancy that you spoke to me of a more distant post," Don Ruiz said.

"Yes; for I fancied San Miguel abandoned, if not in ruins. Before I gave you what might prove a fallacious hope, I wished to assure myself of the truth of the case."

"Do you believe that the Commandant will consent to receive us?" the young lady asked.

"Certainly, Senorita, for a thousand reasons. In the first place, the frontier posts are only established for the purpose of watching over the safety of travellers; and then, again, San Miguel is commanded by one of your relations—or, at any rate, an intimate friend of your family."

The young people looked at each other in surprise.

"Do you know this Commandant's name?" Don Ruiz asked.

"I was told it: he is Don Marcos de Niza."

"Oh!" Dona Mariana exclaimed, joyfully; "I should think we do know him: Don Marcos is a cousin of ours."

"In that case, all is for the best," the hunter answered, coldly. "Let us continue our journey; for there is a cloud of dust behind us that forebodes us no good, if it reaches us before we have entered the post."

The young people, without answering, resumed their gallop, crossed the wood, and entered the little fort.

"Look!" Stronghand said to Don Ruiz and his sister, the moment the gate closed upon them. They turned back. A numerous band of horsemen issued from the wood at this moment, and galloped up at full speed, uttering ferocious yells.

"This is the second time you have saved our lives, Caballero," Dona Mariana said to the partizan, with a look of gratitude.

"Why count them, Senorita?" he replied, with a sadness mingled with bitterness. "Do I do so?"

The maiden gave him a look of undefinable meaning, turned her head away with a blush, and silently followed her brother.

The Spaniards, whatever may be the opinion the Utopians of the old world express about their mode of civilization, and the way in which they treated the Indians of America, understood very well how to enhance the prosperity of the countries they had been endowed with by the strong arms of those heroic adventurers who were called Cortez, Pizarro, Bilboa, Alvarado, &c., and whose descendants, if any by chance exist, are now in the most frightful wretchedness, although their ancestors gave a whole world and incalculable riches to their ungrateful country.

When the Spanish rule was established in America, the first care of the conquerors

—after driving back the Indians who refused to accept their iron yoke into frightful deserts, where they hoped want would put an end to them—was to secure their frontiers, and prevent those indomitable hordes, impelled by hunger and despair, from entering the newly-conquered country and plundering the towns and haciendas. For this purpose they established along the desert line a cordon of presidios and military posts, which were all connected together, and could, in case of need, assist each other, not so much through their proximity—for they were a great distance apart, and scattered over a great space—but by means of numerous patrols of lanceros, who constantly proceeded from one post to the other.

At present, since the declaration of independence, owing to the neglect of the governments which have succeeded each other in this unhappy country, most of the presidios and forts no longer exist. Some have been burned by the Indians, who became invaders in their turn, and are gradually regaining the territory the Europeans took from them; while others have been abandoned, or so badly kept up, that they are for the most part in ruins. Still, here and there you find a few, which exceptional circumstances have compelled the inhabitants to repair and defend.

As these forts were built in all the colonies on the same plan, in describing the post of San Miguel, which still exists, and which we have visited, the reader will easily form an idea of the simple and yet effective defence adopted by the Europeans to protect them from the surprises of their implacable and crafty foes.

The post of San Miguel is composed of four square pavilions, connected together by covered ways, the inner walls of which surround a courtyard planted with lemon-trees, peach-trees, and algarobes. On this court open the rooms intended for travellers, the barracks, &c. The outer walls have only one issue, and are provided with loop-holes, which can only be reached by mounting a platform eight feet high and three wide. All the masonry is constructed of *adobes*, or large blocks of earth stamped and baked in the sun.

Twenty feet beyond this wall is another, formed of cactuses, planted very closely together and having their branches intertwined. This vegetable wall, if we may be allowed the use of the expression, is naturally very thick, and protected by formidable prickles, which render it impenetrable for the half-clad and generally badly-armed Indians. The only entrance to it is a heavy gate, supported by posts securely bedded in the ground. The soldiers, standing at the loop-holes of the second wall, fire in perfect shelter, and command the space above the cactuses.

On the approach of Indians, when the Mexican Moon is at hand—that is to say, the invariable season of their invasions—the sparse dwellers on the border seek refuge inside San Miguel, and there in complete safety wait till their enemies are weary of a siege which can have no result for them, or till they are put to flight by soldiers sent from a town frequently fifty leagues off.

Don Marcos de Niza was a man of about forty, short and plump, but withal active and quick. His regular features displayed a simplicity of character, marked with intelligence and decision. He was one of those educated honest professional officers, of whom the Mexican army unfortunately counts too few in its ranks. Hence, as he thoroughly attended to his duties, and had never tried to secure promotion by intrigue and party manœuvres, he had remained a captain for ten years past, without hope of promotion, in spite of his qualifications (which were recognised and appreciated by all) and his irreproachable conduct. The post he occupied at this moment as Commandant of the Block-house of San Miguel proved the value the Governor of the province set upon him; for the frontier posts, constantly exposed to the attacks of the Redskins, can only be given to sure men, who have long been accustomed to Indian warfare.

CHAPTER IV.

THE POST OF SAN MIGUEL.

As the dangerous honour of commanding one of the border forts like San Miguel is not at all coveted by the brilliant officers accustomed to clatter their sabres on the stones of the Palace in Mexico, it is generally only given to brave soldiers who have no prospect of promotion left to them.

Informed by a cabo, or corporal, of the names of the guests who thus suddenly arrived, the Captain rose to meet them with open arms and a smile on his lips.

"Oh, oh," he exclaimed, gleefully; "this is a charming surprise! Children, I am delighted to see you."

"Do not thank us, Don Marcos," Dona Mariana answered, smilingly. "We are not paying you a visit, but have come to ask shelter and protection of you."

"You have them already. Rayo de Dios! are we not relations, and very close ones, too?"

"Without doubt, cousin," Don Ruiz said; "hence, in our misfortune, it is a great happiness for us to come across you."

"Hilloh! you have something serious to tell me," the Captain continued, his face growing gloomy.

"So serious," the young man said, with a bow to the partizan, who stood motionless by his side, "that, had it not been for the help of this caballero, in all probability we should be lying dead in the desert."

"Oh, oh; my poor children! Come, dismount and follow me; you must need rest and refreshment after such an alarm. Cabo Hernandez, take charge of the horses."

The corporal took the horses, which he led to the corral; and the young people followed the Captain, after having been kissed and hugged by him several times. Don Marcos pressed the hunter's hand, and made him a sign to follow them.

"There," he said, after introducing his guests into a room modestly furnished with a few butaccas; "sit down, children; and when you have rested, we will talk."

Refreshments had been prepared on a table. While the young people enjoyed them, the Captain quitted them, and went with the hunter into another room. So soon as they were alone, the two men became serious, and the joy that illumined the Captain's face was suddenly extinguished.

"Well," he asked Stronghand, after making him a sign to sit down, "what news?"

"Bad," he answered, distinctly.

"I expected it," the officer muttered, with a sad toss of the head; "we must put on our harness again, and push out into the savannah, in order to prove to these bandits that we are able to punish them."

The hunter shook his head several times, but said nothing. The Captain looked at him attentively for some minutes.

"What is the matter, my friend?" he at length asked him, with growing anxiety; "I never saw you so sad and gloomy before."

"The reason is," he answered, "because circumstances have never been so serious."

"Explain yourself, my friend; I confess to you that you are really beginning to alarm me. With the exception of a few insignificant marauders, the borders have never appeared to me more quiet."

"It is a deceitful calm, Don Marcos, which contains the tempest in its bosom—and a terrible tempest, I assure you."

"And yet our spies are all agreed in assuring us that the Indians are not at all thinking of an expedition."

"It proves that your spies betray you, that's all."

"Possibly so; but still, I should like some proof or sign."

"I ask for nothing better; I am enabled to give you the most positive information."

"Very good; that is the way to speak. I am listening to you."

"Before all, is your garrison strong?"

"I consider it large enough."

"Perhaps so; how many men have you?"

"Sixty or seventy, about."

"That is not enough."

"What! not enough? The garrisons of block-houses are never more numerous."

"In a time of peace, it may be so; but under present circumstances, I repeat to you, that they are not enough, and you will soon agree with me on that score. You must send off a courier, without the loss of a moment, to ask for a reinforcement of from one hundred and fifty to two hundred men. Do not deceive yourself, Captain; you will be the first attacked, and the attack will be a rude one. I warn you."

"Thanks for the hint. Still, my good friend, you will permit me not to follow it till you have proved to me that there are urgent reasons for doing so."

"As you please, Captain; you are the commandant of the post, and your responsibility must urge you to prudence. I will therefore abstain from making any further observations on a subject which only concerns me very indirectly."

"You are annoyed, and wrongly so, my friend; the responsibility to which you refer demands that I should not let myself be led by vague rumours to take measures I might have cause to regret. Give me the explanation I expect of you; and, probably, when I know the imminence of the danger that threatens me, I shall follow your advice."

"I wish for nothing more than to satisfy you; so listen to me. What I have to tell you will not take long."

At this moment the room door opened,

and Corporal Hernandez appeared. The Captain, annoyed at being thus inopportunely disturbed, turned sharply round and angrily addressed the man—

"Well, Corporal," he said, "what the fiend do you want now?"

"Excuse me, Captain," the poor fellow said, astounded at this rough greeting, "but the Lieutenant sent me."

"Well, what does the Lieutenant want? Speak! but be brief, if that is possible."

"Captain, the sentry has seen a large party of .horsemen coming at full gallop towards the fort, and the Lieutenant ordered me to warn you."

"Eh," said the Captain, looking uneasily at the hunter, "were you in the right? and is this troop the vanguard of the enemy you threaten us with?"

"This troop," the hunter answered, with an equivocal smile, "has been following Don Ruiz and myself since the morning. I do not believe that these horsemen are Indians."

"What's the Lieutenant's opinion about these scamps?" the Captain asked the Corporal.

"They are too far off yet, and too hidden

by the dust they raise, Captain, for it to be possible to recognise them," the non-commissioned officer replied, with a bow.

"That is true. We had better, I believe, go and look for ourselves. Will you come?"

"I should think so," the hunter said, as he seized his rifle, which he had deposited in a corner of the room; and they went out.

Don Ruiz and his sister were talking together, while doing ample justice to the refreshment placed at their disposal. On seeing the Captain, the young man rose and walked up to him.

"Cousin," he said to him, with a bow, "I hear that you are on the point of being attacked; and as it is to some extent my cause you are going to defend, for the bandits who threaten you at this moment are allies of those with whom I had a fight last night, pray allow me to fire a shot by your side."

"Viva Dios! Most heartily, my dear cousin," the Captain answered, gaily; "although these scoundrels are not worth the trouble. Come along!"

"That's a fine fellow!" the Captain whispered in the hunter's ear.

The latter made no answer. He contented

himself with shrugging his shoulders, and turned away.

"Oh," Dona Mariana exclaimed, "Ruiz, what are you going to do? Stay with me, I implore you, brother."

"Impossible, sister," the young man answered, as he kissed her; "what would our cousin think of me were I to skulk here when fighting was going on?"

"Fear nothing, Nina; I am answerable for your brother," the Captain said with a smile.

The girl sat down again sadly on the butacca from which she had risen, and the four men then left the room, and proceeded to the *patio*, or court. Here everybody was busy. The Lieutenant, an old experienced soldier, with a grey moustache and face furrowed by sabre-cuts, and whose whole life had been spent on the borders, had not lost his time. While, by his order, Corporal Hernandez warned the Captain, he had ordered the "fall-in" to be beaten, had placed the best shots at the loop-holes, and made all arrangements to avoid a surprise and give a warm reception to the enemy who advanced so daringly against the fort.

When the Captain set foot in the court, he stopped, embraced at a glance the wise and intelligent arrangements made by his Lieutenant, and a smile of satisfaction spread over his features.

"And now," he said to the hunter, "let us go and see who the enemy is with whom we have to deal."

"It is unnecessary; for I can tell you, Captain," the other replied; "they are the pirates."

"Pirates!" Don Marcos exclaimed in amazement. "What! those villains would dare——"

"Alone, certainly not," Stronghand quickly interrupted him; "but with the certainty of being supported by the Indians, of whom they are only the vanguard, they will not hesitate to do so. However, unless I am greatly mistaken, their attack will not be serious; and their object is probably to discover in what state of defence the post is. Receive them, then, in such a way as to leave them no doubt on this head, and prove to them that you are perfectly on your guard; and this demonstration will without doubt be sufficient to send them flying."

"You are right," said the Captain. "Viva

Dios! they shall have their answer, I promise you."

He then gave the Corporal an order in a low voice; the latter bowed, and went off hurriedly. For some minutes a deep silence prevailed in the fort. The moments that precede a contest bring with them something solemn, which causes the bravest men to reflect, and prepare for the struggle, either by a powerful effort of the will, or by mentally addressing a last and fervent prayer to Heaven.

All at once, horrible yells were heard, mingled with the furious galloping of many horses; and then the enemy appeared, leaning over the necks of their steeds, and brandishing their weapons with an air of defiance. When they came within pistol-shot, the word to fire was given from the walls, and a general discharge burst forth like a clap of thunder.

The horsemen fell into confusion, and turned back precipitately and in the greatest disorder, followed by the Mexican bullets, which, directed by strong arms and sure eyes, made great ravages in their ranks at every step. Still, they had not fled so fast but that they could be recognised for what they really were—that is, pirates of the prairies. Half naked for the most part, and without saddles, they brandished their rifles and long lances, and excited their horses by terrific yells.

Two or three individuals, probably chiefs, with their heads covered by a species of turban, were noticeable through their ragged uniforms, doubtless torn off murdered soldiers; their repulsive dirt and ferocious appearance inspired the deepest disgust. No doubt was possible: these wretches were certainly whites and half-breeds. What a difference between these sinister bandits and the Apaches, Comanches, and Arapahoes—those magnificent children of nature, so careful in the choice of their weapons—so noble in their demeanour.

After a rather long race, they stopped to hold counsel, out of range of the firearms. They were at this moment joined by a second band, whose leader began speaking and gesticulating with the utmost excitement, pointing to the fort each moment with his rifle. The two bands, united, might possibly amount to one hundred and fifty horsemen.

After a rather long discussion, the pirates

started agaiu, and stopped at the very foot of the walls. Captain Niza, wishing to inflict a severe chastisement on them, had given orders not to fire, but to let them do as they pleased. Hidden by the thick cactus hedge, the bandits had suddenly become invisible; but the Mexicans, confiding in the strength of their position and the solidity of the posts and gates, felt no fear.

Reassured by the silence of the garrison, some thirty pirates, among whom were several of their chiefs, escaladed the great gate in turn, and rushed toward the second wall. Unluckily for the success of their plan, the wall was too lofty to be cleared in the same way; hence they scattered. Some sought stones and posts to beat in the second gate; while others tried, though in vain, to open the one they had so easily scaled.

The Mexicans could distinctly hear the pirates in the second *enceinte* explaining to their comrades the difficulty they experienced in penetrating into the fort, and they must force the gate, in order to allow a passage for those who remained outside. The latter then threw their *reatas*, which, caught upon the posts, were tightened by the combined efforts of the men and horses, and seemed on the point of pulling the gate off its hinges; but the posts held firmly, and were not even shaken by this supreme effort.

"What are you waiting for, Captain?" Don Ruiz whispered in the Commandant's ear. "Why do you not kill these vermin?"

"There are not enough yet in the trap," he answered, with a cunning look; "let them come."

In fact, as if the bandits had wished to obey the old soldier, some twenty more clambered over the gate, so that there were fifty of the pirates between the cactus and the stone wall. Encouraged by their numbers, which momentarily increased, they made a general assault. But, all at once, every loop-hole was lit up by a sinister flash, and the bullets began showering uninterruptedly on the wretches, who, through their own position, found it impossible to answer the plunging fire of the Mexicans. Recognising the fault they had committed, and the trap they had so stupidly entered, the pirates became demoralized, fear seized upon them, and they only thought of flight.

Then they dashed at the outer gate, to clamber over it and reach the plain; and there the bullets dashed them down again—suffering from a desperation which was the greater because they had no help to hope for from their friends outside, whom, at the first check, they had heard start off at full speed; and consequently they felt they were lost.

The Mexicans, pitiless in their vengeance, fired incessantly on the wretches, some of whom, by crawling on their hands and knees, succeeded in reaching the foot of the wall below the loop-holes—a position in which they could not be attacked, unless the Mexicans exposed themselves, and ran the risk of being killed or wounded. Of fifty bandits who had scaled the gate, fourteen still lived; the others were dead, and not one had succeeded in making his escape.

"Ha! ha!" said the Captain, rubbing his hands gleefully. "I fancy that the lesson will be useful, though it may have been a trifle rough."

But, on the reiterated entreaties of Don Ruiz, the worthy Commandant, who in his heart was not cruel, consented to ask the survivors if they were willing to surrender, a proposition which the pirates greeted with yells of rage and defiance. These fourteen men, though their rifles were discharged, were not enemies to despise, armed as they were with long and heavy *machetes*, and resolved to die. The Mexicans were acquainted with them, and knew that in a hand-to-hand fight they would prove tough customers.

Still there must be an end to it. At an order from the Captain the gate of the second wall was suddenly opened, and some twenty horsemen charged at full gallop the bandits, who, far from recoiling, awaited them with a firm foot. The *mêlée* was terrible, but short. Three Mexicans were killed, and five others seriously wounded; but the pirates, after an obstinate resistance, fell never to rise again.

Only one of them—profiting by the disorder and the attention which the soldiers remaining at the loop-holes paid to the fight—succeeded by a miracle of resolution and strength in scaling the wall and flying. This pirate, the only one who escaped the massacre, was Kidd. On reaching the plain he stopped for a second, turned to the fort with a gesture of menace and defiance, and, leaping on a riderless horse, went off amid a shower of bullets, not one of which struck him.

CHAPTER V.

THE STAY IN THE FOREST.

When the fight was over, and order restored at the post, the Captain bade his Lieutenant have the bodies lying on the battle-field picked up and hung by the feet to the trees on the plain, so that they might become the prey of wild beasts, though not until they had been decapitated. The heads were to remain exposed on the walls of the forts, and act as an object of terror to the bandits, who, after this act of summary justice, would not venture to approach the neighbourhood of the post.

Then, when all these orders had been given, the Commandant returned to his residence, where Don Ruiz had already preceded him in order to reassure his sister as to the result of the fight. Don Marcos was radiant: he had gained a great advantage—

at least he thought so — over the border ruffians; he had inflicted on them an exemplary punishment at the expense of an insignificant loss, and supposed that for a long time no one would venture to attack the post entrusted to him.

Unfortunately, the woodranger was not of the same opinion: each time the Captain smiled and rubbed his hands at the recollection of some episode in the fight, Stronghand shook his head sadly, and frowned anxiously. This was done so frequently, that at last the worthy Commandant was compelled to take notice of it.

"What's the matter with you now?" he asked him, with an air half vexed, half pleased. "You are, on my soul, the most extraordinary man I know. Nothing satisfies you; you are always in a bad temper. Hang it! I do not know how to treat you. Did we not give those scoundrels a remarkable thrashing, eh? Come, answer!"

"I allow it," the hunter replied laconically.

"Hum! It is lucky you allow so much. And yet they fought bravely, I fancy."

"Yes; and it is that which frightens me."

"I do not understand you."

"Was I not giving you important information when we were interrupted by the Cabo Hernandez?"

"That is to say, you were going to give it me."

"Yes; and with your permission, now that we have no fear of being interrupted for a while, I will impart the news to you."

"I ask nothing better; although I suppose that the defeat the pirates have experienced must deprive the news of much of its importance."

"The pirates play but a very small part in what I have to tell you."

"Speak, then! I know that you are too earnest a man to try and amuse yourself at my expense by inspiring me with ridiculous alarm."

"You shall judge for yourself the perils of the situation in which you may find yourself at any moment, if you do not employ the greatest precaution and the most excessive prudence."

The two men seated themselves on butaccas, and the Commandant, who was more excited than he wished to show by this startling preamble, made the hunter a sign to commence his revelations.

"About two months ago," the latter began, "I was at the Presidio of San Estevan, whither certain personal matters had called me. This Presidio, which, as you know, is about two days' journey from here, is very important, and serves to some extent in connecting all the posts scattered along the Indian border."

The Captain gave a nod of assent.

"I am," the hunter continued, "on rather intimate terms with Don Gregorio Ochova, the Colonel commanding the Presidio, and during my last stay at San Estevan I had opportunities for seeing him rather frequently. You know the savageness of my character, and the species of instinctive repulsion with which anything resembling a town inspires me: hence, I need hardly say, that no sooner was my business ended than I made preparations to depart, and, according to my custom, intended to leave the Presidio at a very early hour. I did not like to go away without saying good-bye to the Colonel and shaking hands with him; so I went to his house for the purpose of taking leave. I found him in a state of extreme agitation, walking up and down, and apparently affected by a violent passion or great anxiety. On seeing me, he uttered an exclamation of delight, and ran up to me, exclaiming,—

"'Oh, Stronghand! where on earth have you been hiding? I have been seeking you everywhere for the last two hours, and have put a dozen soldiers on your heels, who could not possibly find you.'

"I looked at the Colonel in surprise.

"'You were seeking for me, Don Gregorio? I assure you that I was close to you, and very easy to find.'

"'It seems not. But here you are—that is the main point; and I care little where you were, or what you were doing. Do you think about making any lengthened stay at San Estevan?'

"'No, Colonel,' I answered at once, 'my affairs are settled; I intend to start at an early hour to-morrow, and I have just come to say good-bye, and thank you for the hospitality you have shown me during my stay at the Presidio.'

"'Good!' he said, eagerly, 'that is all for the best; but,' he added, recollecting himself, and taking my hand in a kindly way, 'do not suppose that it is my desire to see you depart that makes me speak thus.'

"'I am convinced of the contrary,' I remarked with a bow.

"He continued,—

"'You can, Stronghand, do me a great service, if you will.'

"'I am at your command.'

"'This is the matter,' he said, at once entering on the business. 'For some days past, the most alarming reports have been spreading through the Presidio, though it is impossible to find out their origin.'

"'And what may they be?' I asked.

"'It is said—(notice, I say it is said, and affirm nothing, as I know nothing positive) —it is said, then, that a general uprising against us is preparing—that the Indians, laying aside for a moment their private hatreds, and forgetting their clannish quarrels to think only of the hereditary hatred they entertain for us, are combining to attempt a general attack on the posts, which they purpose to destroy, in order to devastate our borders more freely. Their object is said to be, not only the destruction of the posts, but also the invasion of several States, such as Sonora and Cinaloa, in which they intend to establish themselves permanently after expelling us.'

" 'The reports are serious,' I remarked, 'but nothing has as yet happened to confirm their truth.'

" 'That is true; but you know that there is always a certain amount of truth in every vague rumour, and it is that truth I should like to know.'

" 'Is no nation mentioned by name among those which are to take up arms?'

" 'Yes; more particularly the Papayos—that is to say, the grand League of the Apaches, Axuas, Gilenos, Comanches, Mayos, and Opatas. But the more serious thing is, always according to the report, that the white and half-bred marauders on the border are leagued with them, and mean to help them in their expedition against us.'

" 'That is really serious,' I answered; 'but, pardon me for questioning you, Colonel; what do you purpose doing to make head against the imminent danger that threatens you?'

" 'That is exactly why I want you, my friend; and you would do me a real service by assisting me in this affair.'

" 'I am ready to do anything that depends on myself to oblige you.'

" 'I was certain of that answer, my friend.

This is the matter, then. You understand that I cannot remain thus surrounded by vague rumours and terrors that have no apparent cause, but still carry trouble into families and cause perturbation in trade. During the last few weeks, especially, various serious events have given a certain consistency to these rumours—travellers have been murdered, and several valuable waggon-trains plundered, almost at the gates of the Presidio. It is time for this state of things to cease, and for us to know definitively the truth or falsehood of the rumours; for this purpose I require a brave, devoted man, thoroughly acquainted with Indian manners and customs, who would consent——'

"I interrupted him quickly.

"'I understand what you want, Colonel; seek no further, for I am the man you stand in need of. To-morrow at sunrise I will start: and within two months I pledge myself to give you the most explicit information, and tell you what you may have to fear, and what truth there is in all that is being said around you.'

"The Colonel thanked me warmly, and the next morning I set out on my tour of investigation, as we had arranged."

"Well," the Captain exclaimed, who had followed this long story with ever increasing interest; "and what information have you picked up?"

"This information," the hunter answered, "is of a nature far more serious than even public report had said. The situation is most critical, and not a moment must be lost in preparing for defence. I was going to San Estevan, where Colonel Don Gregorio must be awaiting my return with the utmost impatience, when I thought of seeing whether the Post of San Miguel, which had so long been unoccupied, had received a garrison. That is how chance, my dear Captain, made us meet here when I thought I should see you at the Presidio."

The Captain shook his head thoughtfully. "A month ago," he said, "Don Gregorio ordered me to come here and hold my ground, though he did not inform me of the motives that compelled him so suddenly to place San Miguel in a state of defence."

"Well; now you know the reasons."

"Yes; and I thank you for having told me. But, between ourselves, are matters so serious as you lead me to suppose?"

"A hundred times more so. I have traversed the desert in all directions; I have been present at the meetings of the chiefs—in a word, I know the most private details of the expedition that is preparing."

"*Viva Dios!* I will not let myself be surprised—be at your ease about that; but you were right in advising me to ask for help, as my garrison is too weak to resist a well-arranged assault. This morning's attack has made me reflect; so I will immediately——"

"Do not take the trouble," the hunter interrupted him; "I will act as your express."

"What! are you going to leave us at once?"

"I must, my dear Captain; for I have to give Don Gregorio an account of the mission he confided to me. Reflect what mortal anxiety he must feel at not seeing me return."

"That is true. In spite of the lively pleasure I should feel in keeping you by me, I am compelled to let you go. When do you start?"

"This moment."

"Already?"

"My horse has rested; there are still five

or six hours of daylight left, and I will take advantage of them."

He made a movement to leave the room.

"You have not said good-bye to Don Ruiz and his sister," the Captain observed.

The hunter stopped, his brows contracted, and he seemed to be reflecting.

"No," he said, ere long, "it would make me lose precious time. You will make my apologies to them, Captain. Moreover," he added, with a bitter smile, "our acquaintance is not sufficiently long, I fancy, for Don Ruiz and his sister to attach any great importance to my movements, so for the last time, good-bye."

"I will not press you," the Captain answered; "do as you please. Still, it would have perhaps been more polite to take leave."

"Nonsense," he said, ironically; "am I not a savage? Why should I employ that refinement of politeness which is only customary among civilized people?"

The Captain contented himself with shrugging his shoulders as an answer, and they went out. Five minutes later the hunter was mounted.

"Do not fail to report to the Colonel,"

Don Marcos said, "what happened here today; and above all, ask him for assistance."

"All right, Captain; and do not you go to sleep."

"*Caraï*—I shall feel no inclination. So now, good-bye, and good luck!"

"Good-bye, and many thanks."

They exchanged a last shake of the hand, the hunter galloped out into the plain, and the Captain returned to his house, muttering to himself,

"What a strange man! Is he good or bad? Who can say?"

When the supper hour arrived, the two young people, astonished at the hunter's absence, asked after him of the Captain. When the latter told them of his departure, they felt grieved and hurt at his having gone without bidding them farewell; and Dona Mariana especially was offended at such unaccountable behaviour on the part of a caballero; for which, in her desire to excuse him, she in vain sought a reason. Still they did not show their feelings, and the evening passed very pleasantly.

At the hour for retiring, Don Ruiz, more than ever eager to rejoin his father, reminded the Captain of the offer of service he had made him, and asked for an escort, in order to continue his journey on the morrow; but Don Marcos answered with a peremptory refusal, that not only would he give no escort, but he insisted on his relations remaining temporarily under his guard.

Don Ruiz naturally asked an explanation of his cousin; which he did not hesitate to give, by telling them of the conversation between himself and the hunter. Don Ruiz and his sister had been too near death to expose themselves again to the hazards of a long journey in the desert alone, and unable to offer any effectual defence against such persons as thought proper to attack them; still the young man, annoyed at this new delay, asked the Captain at what period they might hope to regain their liberty.

"Oh! your seclusion will not be long," the latter replied with a smile; "so soon as I have received the reinforcements I expect from San Estevan—that is to say, in seven or eight days at the most—I will pick you out an escort, and you can be off."

Don Ruiz, forced to satisfy himself with this promise, thanked him warmly; and the young people made their arrangements to pass the week in the least wearisome way possible. But life is very dull at a frontier post, especially when you are expecting a probable attack from the Indians, and when, consequently, all the gates are kept shut, when sentries are stationed all around, and the only amusement is to look out on the plain through the loop-holes.

The Captain, justly alarmed by the news the hunter had given him, had made the best arrangements his limited resources allowed to resist any attack from the Indians, if they appeared before the succour arrived from San Estevan. By his orders all the rancheros and small landowners established within a radius of fifteen leagues had been warned of an approaching invasion, and received an invitation to take shelter within the post.

The majority, recognising the gravity of this communication, hastened to pack up their furniture and most valuable articles; and, driving before them their horses and cattle, hurried from all sides at once to the fort, with a precipitation which proved the profound terror the Indians inspired them with. In this way, the interior of San Miguel was soon encumbered with young men and old men, women, and children, and cattle—most of whom, unable to find lodgings in the houses, were forced to bivouac in the yards; which, however, was but a trifling inconvenience to them in a country where it hardly ever rains, and where the nights are not cold enough to render sleeping in the open air unpleasant.

The Captain organized this heterogeneous colony to the best of his ability. The women, children, and old men were sheltered under tents or *jacals* made of branches, to protect them from the copious morning dew, while all the men capable of bearing arms were exercised, so as in case of attack to assist in the common defence.

But this enormous increase of population required an enormous stock of provisions; and hence the Captain sent out numerous patrols for the purpose of procuring the required corn and cattle. Don Ruiz took advantage of this to make excursions in the vicinity; while his sister, in the company of young girls of her own age, of whom several had entered the fort with their families, tried to forget, or rather cheat, the weariness of their seclusion.

The appearance of the post had completely changed; and, thanks to the Captain's intelligence, ten days after the hunter's departure San Miguel had become a really formidable fortress. Large trenches had been dug, and barricades erected; but, unfortunately, the garrison, though numerous enough to resist a sudden attack, was too weak to sustain a long siege.

One morning, at sunrise, the sentries signalized a thick cloud of dust advancing toward the post with the headlong speed of a whirlwind. The alarm was immediately given; the walls were lined with soldiers; and preparations were made to resist these men, who, though invisible, were supposed to be enemies.

Suddenly, on coming within gunshot, the horsemen halted, the dust dispersed, and the garrison perceived with delight that all these men wore the Mexican uniform. A quarter of an hour later, eighty lanceros, each carrying an infantry-man behind him, entered the fort, amid the deafening shouts of the garrison and the farmers who had sought refuge behind the walls. It was the succour requested by the Captain, and sent off from San Estevan by Colonel Don Gregorio.

CHAPTER VI.

A GLANCE AT THE PAST.

In Spanish America, and especially in Peru and Mexico, all the Creoles of the pure white breed pretend to be descended in a straight line from the first Conquistadors. We have no need to discuss this claim, whose falsehood is visible to any man at all conversant with the sanguinary history of the numberless civil wars—a species of organized massacre—which followed the establishment of the Spaniards in these rich countries.

Still there are in America some families, very few in number it is true, which can justly boast of this glorious origin. Most of these families live on the estates conceded to their ancestors—they only marry among themselves, and only interfere against the grain in the political events of the day. With their eyes turned to the past, which is so full of great memories for them, they have kept up the old traditions of the chivalrous loyalty of the time of Charles V., which are forgotten everywhere else. They maintain the national honour unsullied, and those patriarchal virtues of the old time which they alone still practise with a proud and simple majesty.

The Creoles, half-breeds, and Indians, in spite of the hatred they affect for their old masters, and the principles of so-called republican equality which they profess with such absurd emphasis in the presence of strangers, feel for these families a respect bordering on veneration; for they seem to understand inwardly the superiority of these powerful natures, which no political convulsion has been able to level or even bind, over their own vicious decrepit natures, which have grown old without ever having been young.

A few leagues from Arispe, the old capital of the Intendancy of Sonora, but now greatly fallen, and only a second-class city, there stands like an eagle's nest, on the summit of an abrupt rock, a magnificent showy mansion, whose strong and haughty walls are crowned with *Almenas*, which at the time of the Spanish conquest were only permitted to families of the old and pure nobility, and they alone had the right to have battlements on their houses.

This fortress-palace—which dates from the first days of the conquest, and whose antiquity is written on its walls, which have seen so many bullets flatten, so many arrows break against them, but which time, that grand destroyer of the most solid things, is gradually crumbling away by a continuous effort, under the triple influences of the air, the sun, and rain—has never changed masters since the day of its construction, and the chiefs of the same family, on dying, have ever left it to their descendants.

This family is one of those to which we just now referred, whose origin dates back to the first conquerors, and whose name is Tobar de Moguer—(Moguer was added at a later date, doubtless in memory of the Spanish town whence the chief of the family came.)

In 1541, Don Antonio de Mendoça, Viceroy of New Spain, organized the expedition to Cibola, a mysterious country, visited a few years previously by Alvaro Nunez, Cabeça of Vaca, and about which the most marvellous and extraordinary reports were spread, all the better suited to inflame the avarice and unextinguishable thirst for gold by which the Spanish adventurers were devoured.

The expedition, consisting of 300 Spaniards and 800 Indian allies, started from Compostella, the capital of New Galicia, on April 17, 1541, under the orders of Don Francisco Vasquez Coronado. The officers nominated by the Viceroy were all gentlemen of distinction; among them as standard bearer was Don Pedro de Tobar, whose father, Don Fernando de Tobar, had been Majordomo-Major in the reign of Jane the Mad, mother of the Emperor Charles V.

We will only say a few words about this expedition, the preparations for which were immense; and which would have doubtless furnished better results, and proved to the advantage of all, had the chief thought less of the immense fortune he left behind in New Spain, and more of the immense responsibility weighing upon him.

After innumerable fatigues, the expedition reached Cibola, which, instead of being the rich and magnificent city they expected to see, was only a wretched insignificant village, built on a rock, and which the Spaniards seized after an hour's fighting. Still, the Indians defended themselves bravely, and several Spaniards were wounded. The General himself, hurled down by a stone, would have been infallibly killed, had it not been for the devotion of Don Pedro de Tobar and another officer, who threw themselves before him, and gave their chief time to rise and withdraw from the fight.

The Spaniards, half discouraged by the extraordinary fatigue they were forced to endure, and the continual deceptions that awaited them at every step, but still urged on by that spirit of adventure which never deserted them, resolved after the capture of Cibola to push further on and try their fortunes once again. Thus they reached, with extreme difficulty, the last country visited by the Cabeça de Vaca, to which he had given the name of the Land of Hearts (*tierra de los Corazones*)—not, as might be supposed, because the inhabitants had seemed so gentle and amiable, but solely because, at the period of his passing, the only food they offered him had been stags' hearts.

On reaching this place the Spaniards halted. Don Tristan d'Arellano, who had taken the command of the army in place of

Don Francisco Coronado, who was ailing from the wound received at Cibola, seeing the rich and fertile appearance of this country, resolved to found a town, which he called San Hieronimo de los Corazones. This town was, however, almost immediately abandoned by the Spaniards, who carried the various elements further, and started a new town, to which they gave the name of Senora, afterwards corrupted into Sonora, which eventually became the name of the province.

During this long expedition Don Pedro de Tobar distinguished himself on several occasions. At the head of seventeen horsemen, four foot soldiers, and a Franciscan monk of the name of Fray Juan de Padella, who in his youth had been a soldier, Don Pedro de Tobar discovered the province of Tutaliaco, which contained several towns, the houses being of several storeys. All these towns, or rather villages, were carried by storm by Don Pedro, and the province was subjugated in a few days.

When, twenty years after, the Viceroy wishing to recompense Don Pedro's services, offered him estates, the latter, who held Sonora in pleasant recollection, asked that land should be granted him in this province, which reminded him of the prowess of his youth, and to which he was attached by the very fatigues he had undergone and the dangers he had incurred. During the twenty years that had elapsed since Coronado's expedition, Don Pedro had married the daughter of Don Rodrigo Maldonado, brother-in-law of the Duke of Infantado, and one of his old comrades in arms. As Don Rodrigo had settled in Sonora, Don Pedro, in order to be near him, took up his abode on the site of Cibola, which had long been destroyed and abandoned, and built on the crest of the rock the magnificent Hacienda del Toro, which, as we have said, remained for centuries in the family, with the immense estates dependent on it.

Like all first-class haciendas in Mexico, El Toro was rather a town than a simple habitation, according to the idea formed in Europe of private estates. It comprised all the old territory of Cibola. On all sides its lofty walls, built on the extremity of the rock, hung over the abyss. It contained princely apartments for the owners, a chapel, workshops of every description, store-houses, barracks, quarters for the pious, and carals for the horses and cattle, with an immense *huerta*, planted with the finest trees and the most fragrant flowers. In a word, it was, and probably still is, one of those gigantic abodes which appear built for Titans, and of which the finest feudal châteaus in the Old World offer but an imperfect idea.

The fact is, that at the time when the conquerors built these vast residences, inhabitants were sparse in these countries, as is indeed the case now. The owners having their elbows at liberty, could take what land they liked, and hence each ultimately became, without creating any surprise, possessors of a territory equal in size to one of our counties.

It was in 1811, twenty-nine years before the period when our story begins, at the dawn of that glorious Mexican revolution the first cry of which had been raised on the night of September 16, 1810, by Hidalgo—at that time a simple parish priest in the wretched town of Dolores, and whose success, sixteen months later, was so compromised by the disastrous battle of Calderon, in which countless bands of fanatic Indians were broken by the discipline of the old Spanish troops—that the most sensible men regarded it as an unimportant insurrection—a fatal error which caused the ruin of the Spanish domination.

But on November 25, 1811, the day on which we begin this narrative, the insurgents had not yet been conquered at Calderon; on the contrary, their first steps had been marked by successes; from all sides Indians came to range themselves beneath their banner, and their army, badly disciplined, it is true, but full of enthusiasm, amounted to 80,000 men. Already master of several important towns, Hidalgo assembled all his forces with the evident design of dealing a great blow, and generalizing the insurrection, which had hitherto been confined to two provinces.

About two in the afternoon, that is to say, the time when in these climes the heat is most oppressive, a horseman, mounted on a magnificent mustang, was following at a gallop the banks of a small stream, half dried up by the torrid heat of the southern sun, and by whose side a few sickly cotton-wood trees were withering.

The dust, reduced to impalpable atoms, formed a dense cloud round the horseman, who, plunged into sad and gloomy thought, with pale forehead and brows contracted till they touched, continued his journey without noticing the desolate aspect of the country he was traversing, and the depressing calm that prevailed around him. In fact, an utter silence brooded over this desert: the birds had hidden themselves gasping under the foliage, and no other sound could be heard save the shrill, harsh cry of the grasshoppers, which occupied in countless myriads the calcined grass that bordered the road, or rather the track, the traveller was following.

This rider appeared to be about twenty-five years of age; his features were handsome, his glance proud, and the expression of his face haughty, although marked with kindness and courtesy. He was tall and well built; his gestures, which were pleasing, though not stiff, indicated a man who, through his position in the world, was accustomed to a certain deference, and to win the respect of those who surrounded him. His dress had nothing remarkable about it: it was that usually worn by wealthy Spaniards when travelling; still a short sword in a silver sheath and with a curiously-carved hilt, the only weapon he openly carried, showed him to be a gentleman; besides, his complexion, clearer than that of the Creoles, left no doubt as to his Spanish origin.

This horseman, who had left Arispe at sunrise, had been travelling, up to the moment we join him, without stopping or appearing to notice the stifling heat that made the perspiration run down his cheek—so deep was he in thought. On reaching a spot where the track he was following turned sharply to the left, his horse suddenly stopped. The rider, thus aroused from his reverie, raised his head and looked before him, with grief, almost despair, in his glance.

He was at the foot of the rock on the summit of which stands the Hacienda del Toro in all its gloomy majesty. For some minutes he gazed with an expression of regret and sorrow at these frowning buildings, which doubtless recalled happy memories. He shook his head several times, a sigh escaped from his over-burdened chest, and, seeming to form a supreme resolution, he said, in a choking voice, "I will go;" and letting his horse feel the spur, he began slowly scaling the narrow path that led to the summit of the rock and the hacienda gate. A violent contest seemed to be going on in his mind: his flexible face changed each moment, and reflected the various feelings that agitated him; several times his clenched hand drew up the bridle, as if he wished to check his horse and turn back. But each time his will was the more powerful; he constantly overcame the instinctive repugnance that seemed to govern him, and he continued his ascent, with his eyes constantly looking ahead, as if he expected to see some one whose presence he feared come round an angle of the track. But he did not see a soul the whole way.

When he reached the hacienda gate, it was open, and the drawbridge lowered; but though he was evidently expected, there was no one to bid him welcome.

"It must be so," he murmured sadly. "I return to my paternal roof, not as a master, but as a stranger, a fugitive—an accursed man, perhaps."

He crossed the drawbridge, the planks of which re-echoed his horse's footfall, and entered the first courtyard. Here, too, there was no one to greet him. He dismounted; but instead of throwing the bridle on his horse's neck, he held it in his hand

and fastened it to a ring in the wall, saying, in a low, concentrated voice—

"Wait for me, my poor Bravo; you, too, are regarded as an accursed one: be patient; we shall doubtless soon set out again."

The noble animal, as if understanding its master's words and sharing in his grief, turned its delicate, intelligent head toward him, and gave a soft and plaintive whine. The young man, after giving a parting glance at his steed, crossed the first yard with a firm and resolute step, and entered a second one considerably larger. At the end of this court two men were standing motionless on the first step of a magnificent marble staircase, apparently leading to the apartments of the master of the hacienda.

On seeing these two men, the young horseman drew himself up; his face assumed a gloomy and ironical expression, and he walked rapidly toward them. They still remained motionless and stiff, with their eyes fixed on him. When he was but a few paces from them, they uncovered by an automatic movement, and bowed ceremoniously.

"The Marquis is waiting for you, Senor Conde," one of them said.

"Very good," the strange visitor answered; "one of you can announce my arrival to his lordship my father, while the other will guide me to the apartment where I am expected."

The two men bowed a second time, and with heads still uncovered, preceded the young man, who followed with a firm and measured tread. On reaching the top of the steps, one of the servants hurried forward, while the second, slightly checking his speed, continued to guide the horseman. When the footsteps of the first man died out in the immense corridors, the face of the second one suddenly lost its indifferent expression, and he turned round, his eyes full of tears.

"Oh, my young master!" he said, in a voice broken by emotion, "what a misfortune! Oh, Heavens! what a misfortune!"

"What?" the young man asked anxiously; "has anything happened to the Marquis? Or is my lady mother ill?"

The old servant shook his head sadly. "No," he answered; "Heaven be blessed! both are in good health: but why did you leave the paternal mansion, your lordship? Alas! now the misfortune is irremediable."

A cloud of dissatisfaction flitted across the young man's forehead.

"What has happened so terrible during my absence, Perote?"

"Does not your excellency know?" the servant asked in amazement.

"How should I know, my friend?" he answered, mildly. "Have you forgotten that I have been absent from the hacienda for two years?"

"That is true, excellency;—forgive me, I had forgotten it. Alas! since the misfortune has burst upon us, my poor head has been so bad."

"Recover yourself, my good fellow," the young man said, kindly. "I know how much you love me. You have not forgotten," he added, with a bitter sorrow, "that your wife, poor Juana, nourished me with her milk. I know nothing; am even ignorant why my father ordered me so suddenly to come hither. The servant who handed me the letter was doubtless unable to tell anything, and, indeed, I should not have liked to question him."

"Alas! excellency," the old servant continued, "I am myself ignorant why you have been summoned to the hacienda; but Hernando, he may know."

"Ah!" said the young man, with a nervous start, "my brother is here, then?"

"Did you not know it?"

"Have I not already told you that I am utterly ignorant of everything connected with this house?"

"Yes, yes, excellency. Don Hernando is here, and has been here a long time. Heaven guard me from saying anything against my master's son; but perhaps it would have been better had he remained at Guadalajara, for all has greatly changed since his arrival. Take care, Sir, for Don Hernando does not love you."

"What do I care for my brother's hatred?" the young man answered, haughtily. "Am I not the elder son?"

"Yes, yes," the old servant repeated, sadly, "you are the elder son; and yet your brother commands here as master. Since his arrival, it seems as if everything belonged to him already."

The young man let his head sink on his chest, and remained for some minutes crushed; but he soon drew himself up, with flashing eye, and gently laid his hand on the old servant's shoulder.

"Perote," he said to him affectionately, "what is the motto of my family?"

"What do you mean, excellency?" the man-servant asked, startled at the singular question his master asked him.

"You do not remember it," the young man continued, with a smile, as he pointed to an escutcheon over a door. "Well; look, what do you read there?"

"What does your excellency want?"

"Read—read, I tell you."

"You know that motto better than I do, as it was given to one of your ancestors by King Don Fernand of Castile himself."

"Yes, Perote, I know it," he replied, in a firm voice; "and since you will not read it, I will repeat it to you. The motto is: 'Everything for honour, no matter what may happen.' That motto dictates my conduct to me; and be assured, Perote, that I will not fail in what it orders me."

"Oh, your excellency, once again take care. I am only a poor servant of your family, but I saw you born, and I tremble as to what may happen in the coming interview."

"Do not be anxious, my old friend," he answered, with an expression of haughty pride, full of nobleness. "Whatever may happen, I will remember not only what I owe to the memory of my ancestors, but also what I owe to myself; and, without going beyond the limits of that obedience and respect those who gave me birth have a right to, I shall be able to defend myself against the accusations which will doubtless be brought against me."

"Heaven grant, Sir, that you may succeed in dissipating the unjust suspicions so long gathering in the minds of your noble parents, and carefully kept up by the man who during your life-time dares to look with an eye of covetousness on your rich inheritance."

"What do I care for this inheritance?" the young man exclaimed, passionately. "I would gladly abandon it entirely to my brother, if he would cease to rob me of a more precious property, which I esteem a hundred times higher—the love of my father and my mother."

Old Perote only answered with a sigh.

"But," the young man continued, "let us not delay any longer. His lordship must be informed of my arrival; and the slight eagerness I seem to display in proceeding to him and obeying his orders will probably be interpreted to my injury by the man who has for so many years conspired my ruin."

"Yes, you are right: we have delayed too long as it is; come, follow me."

"Where are you taking me?" the young man remarked. "My father's apartments are not situated in this part of the hacienda."

"I am not leading your excellency to them," he answered, sorrowfully.

"Where to, then?" he asked, stopping in surprise.

"To the Red Room," the old servant remarked in a low voice.

"Oh!" the young man muttered; "then my condemnation is about to be pronounced."

Perote only answered by a sigh; and his young master, after a moment's hesitation, made him a sign to go on; and he silently followed him, with a slow step that had something almost solemn in it.

CHAPTER VII.

THE FAMILY TRIBUNAL.

The Hacienda del Toro, like many feudal mansions, contained one room which remained constantly closed, and was only opened on solemn occasions. The head of the family was conveyed there to die, and remained on a bed of state till the day of his funeral: and the wife was confined there. There, too, marriage contracts were signed. In a word, all the great acts of life were performed in this room, which inspired the inhabitants of the hacienda with a respect greatly resembling terror; for on the few occasions on which the Marquises de Tobar found themselves compelled to punish any member of their family, it served as the tribunal where the culprit was tried and sentence pronounced.

This room, situated at the end of the

hacienda, was a large hall of oblong shape, paved with alternate large black and white slabs, and lighted by four lofty windows, which only allowed a gloomy and doubtful light to penetrate.

Tapestry, dating from the fourteenth century, and representing with all the simplicity of the age the different episodes of the mournful battle of Xeres—which delivered Spain to the Moors, and in which Don Rodriguo, the last Gothic king, was killed—covered the walls, and imprinted an indescribable character of sepulchral majesty on this cold and mournful hall, which was probably called the "Red Room" from the prevalence of that colour in the tapestry work.

The young Count de Tobar had never entered this room since the day of his birth; and, however far back his thoughts reverted in childhood, he never remembered to have seen it open. Hence, in spite of all his courage, and the firmness with which he had thought it wise to arm himself for this decisive interview with his father, he could not restrain a slight start of fear on learning that his parents were prepared to receive him there.

The folding doors were open, and on reaching the threshold the young man took in the room at a single glance. At one end, on a daïs covered with a *petate*, the Marquis and Marchioness of Tobar were seated, gloomy and silent, beneath a canopy of black velvet with gold fringe and tassels. Candles, lit in tall, many-branched candelabra, in order to overcome the habitual gloom of the room, threw their flickering light on the aged couple, and imparted to their faces an expression of sternness and harshness that probably did not belong to them.

At the foot of the daïs, and almost touching it, stood a young man of three or four-and-twenty, with handsome and distinguished features, whose elegant attire contrasted with the simple dress of the aged couple: this gentleman was Don Hernando de Tobar, younger son of the Marquis. A footman, the same who had preceded the Count in order to announce his arrival to his master, took a step forward on perceiving the young man.

"El Senor Conde, Don Rodolfo de Tobar y Moguer," he said, in a loud and marked voice.

"Show in the Count," the Marquis said, in a voice which, though broken, was still powerful.

The man-servant discreetly retired, and the door closed upon him. The Count walked up to the foot of the daïs: on reaching it, he bowed a second time, then drew himself up, and respectfully awaited till it pleased his father to address him.

So profound a silence prevailed for some minutes in the room, that the hearts of the four persons might have been heard beating in their bosoms. Don Hernando took cunning side-glances at his brother, whom the aged couple examined with a mixture of sadness and severity.

The young Count, as we said, was standing motionless in front of the daïs. His posture was full of nobility, without being in any way provocative: with his right foot in front, his hand on his sword-guard, and the other holding his hat, whose long feather swept the ground, and his head slightly thrown back, he looked straight before him, without any display of arrogance or disdain. He waited, with a brow rather pale, it is true, owing to the internal emotion he felt; but the expression of his features, far from being that of a culprit, was, on the contrary, that of a man convinced of his innocence, and who expects to see his conduct approved rather than blamed.

"You have arrived, then, Senor Conde," the Marquis at length said, sharply.

The young man bowed, but did not answer.

"You did not display any great eagerness in obeying my invitation."

"My lord, I only received very late last night the letter you did me the honour to send me," the Count answered, gently. "This morning before sunrise I mounted my horse, and rode twenty leagues without stopping, so anxious was I to obey you."

"Yes," the Marquis said, ironically, "I know that; for you are a most obedient son —in words, if not otherwise."

"Excuse me, my lord," he replied, respectfully, "but I do not understand to what you deign to allude at this moment."

The old gentleman bit his lips angrily. "It is because we probably no longer speak the same language, Senor Conde," he said, drily; "but I will try to make myself better understood."

There was a silence, during which the Marquis seemed to be reflecting.

"You are the elder son of the family, sir," he presently continued, "and, as such, responsible for its honour, which your ancestors handed down to you unsullied. You are aware of this, I presume?"

"I am, my lord."

"Since your birth your sainted mother and myself have striven to place before you only examples of loyalty; during your childhood we took pleasure in training you in all the chivalrous virtues which for a long succession of centuries have been the dearest appanage of the race of worthies from whom you are descended. We continuously kept before your eyes the noble motto of our family, of which it is so justly proud. How is it, then, sir, that, suddenly forgetting what you owe to our care and the lessons you received from us, you suddenly, without your mother's permission or mine, abandoned without any plausible motive the paternal roof, and that, deaf to the remonstrances and tearful entreaties of your mother, and rebellious against my orders, you have so completely separated your life from ours, that, with the exception of the name you continue to bear, you have become a perfect stranger?"

"My lord!" the young man stammered.

"It is not an accusation I bring against you, Don Rodolfo," the Marquis continued, quickly; "but I expect a frank and honourable explanation of your conduct. But, take care; the explanation must be clear and unreserved."

"My lord," the Count answered, throwing up his head proudly, "my heart reproaches me with nothing: my conduct has been ever worthy of the name I have the honour to bear. My object, in obeying your orders so eagerly, has not been to justify myself, as I am not guilty of any fault, but to assure you of my respect and obedience."

An incredulous smile played round Don Hernando's mouth, and the Marquis continued with the same tone of frigid sternness—

"I expected another answer from you, sir. I hoped to find you eagerly seize the opportunity my kindness offered you to justify yourself in my sight."

"My lord," the young man replied, respectfully but firmly, "in order that the justification you demand may be possible, I must know the charges brought against me."

"I will not press this subject for the present, sir; but since, as you say, you profess such great respect for my orders, I wish to give you an immediate opportunity to prove your obedience to me."

"Oh, speak, father!" the Count exclaimed, warmly; "whatever you may ask of me——"

"Do not be overhasty in pledging yourself, sir," the Marquis coldly interrupted him, "before you know what I am about to ask of you."

"I shall be so happy to prove to you how far from my heart are the intentions attributed to me."

"Be it so, sir. I thank you for those excellent feelings; hence I will not delay in telling you what you must do to reinstate yourself in my good graces."

"Speak,—speak, my lord!"

The old man, cold and impassive, still regarded his son with the same stern look. The Marchioness, restrained by her husband's presence, fixed on the young man eyes filled with tears, without daring, poor mother, to interfere on his behalf. Don Hernando smiled cunningly aside. As for Don Rodolfo, his father's last words had filled him with fear; and in spite of the pleasure he affected, he trembled inwardly, for he instinctively suspected a snare beneath this pretended kindness.

"My son," the Marquis continued, with a slight tinge of sadness in his voice, "your mother and I are growing old. Years count double at our age, and each step brings us nearer the tomb, which will soon open for us."

"Oh, father!" Don Rodolfo exclaimed.

"Do not interrupt me, my son," the Marquis continued, with a commanding gesture. "You are our first-born, the hope of our name and race: you are four-and-twenty years of age; you are handsome, well-built, instructed by us in all the duties of a gentleman: in short, you are an accomplished cavalier, of whom we have just reason to be proud."

The Marquis paused for a little while. Don Rodolfo felt himself growing more and more pale. His eyes turned wildly to his mother, who sorrowfully bowed her head, in order that his anxious glance might not meet hers. He was beginning to understand what sacrifice his father was about to demand of his filial obedience, and he trembled with terror and despair. The old man continued, in a firm and more marked voice—

"Your mother and I, my son, may be called away soon to appear before the Lord; but as I do not wish to repose in the tomb without having the satisfaction of knowing that our name will not die with us, but be continued in our grandchildren—this desire, which I have several times made known to you, my son, the moment has now arrived to realize; and by marrying, you can secure the tranquillity of the few days still left us to spend on this earth."

"Father——"

"Oh, re-assure yourself, Count," the old gentleman continued, pretending to misunderstand his son's meaning. "I do not intend to force on you one of those marriages in which a couple, united against their wish, only too soon hate one another through the instinctive aversion they feel. No; the wife I intend for you has been chosen by your mother and myself with the greatest care. She is young, lovely, rich, and of a nobility almost equal to ours;—in a word, she combines all the qualities necessary not only to render you happy, but also to revive the brilliancy of our house and impart a fresh lustre to it."

"Father!" Don Rodolfo stammered again.

"My son!" the Marquis continued, with a proud intonation in his voice, as if the name he was about to utter must remove all scruples; "my son, be happy, for you are about to marry Dona Aurelia del Torre Azul, cousin in the fifth degree of the Marquis del Valle."

"Oh, my son!" the Marchioness added entreatingly, "this alliance, which your father so dearly desires, will soothe my last days."

The young man was of livid pallor. He tottered, his eyes wandered hesitatingly around, and his hand, powerfully pressed to his heart, seemed trying to stifle its beating.

"You know my will, sir," the Marquis continued, not appearing to perceive his unhappy son's condition. "I hope that you will soon conform to it: and now, as you must be fatigued after a long ride in the great heat of the day, withdraw to your apartments. To-morrow, when you have rested, we will consult as to the means of introducing you to your future wife as soon as possible."

After uttering these words, in the same cold and peremptory tone he employed during the whole interview, the Marquis prepared to rise.

By an effort over himself the young Count succeeded in repressing the storm that was raging in his heart. Affecting a tranquillity he was far from feeling, he took a step forward, and bowed respectfully to the Marquis.

"Pardon me, my lord," he said, in a voice which emotion involuntarily caused to tremble, "but may I say a few words now?"

The old gentleman frowned.

"Did I not say to-morrow, sir?" he answered, dryly.

"Yes, my lord," the young man answered, sadly; "but, alas! if you do not consent to listen to me to-day, to-morrow may be too late."

"Ah!" said the Marquis, biting his lips with a passion that was beginning to break out, "and for what reason, sir?"

"Because, father," the young man said, firmly, "to-morrow I shall have left this house never to re-enter it."

The Marquis gave him a thundering look from under his grey eyelashes.

"Ah, ah!" he exclaimed, "then I was not deceived; what I have been told is really true."

"What have you been told?"

"Do you wish to know?" the old gentleman exclaimed, furiously. "After all, you are right; it is time that this pitiable farce should end."

"Sir,—sir!" the Marchioness said, with deep grief, "remember that he is your son—your first-born!"

"Silence, madam!" the old man said, harshly; "this rebellious son has played with us long enough; the hour of punishment has pealed, and, by Heaven! it shall be terrible and exemplary."

"In God's name, sir," the Marchioness continued, "do not be inexorable to your child. Let me speak to him; perhaps you are too harsh with him, although you love him. I am his mother; I will convince him, and induce him to carry out your wishes: a mother can find words in her heart to soften her son, and make him understand that he ought not to reject his father's orders."

The old man seemed to hesitate for a moment, but immediately recovered.

"Why should I consent to what you ask, madam?" he replied, with a roughness mingled with pity; "do you not know that the sole quality, or rather the sole vice, of his race which this rebellious son has retained is obstinacy? You will get nothing from him."

"Oh, permit me to say, sir," the old lady continued, in a suppliant voice, "he is my son as well as yours. In the name of that love and that unswerving obedience you have ever found in me, I beseech you to let me make a final attempt to break his resistance, and lead him penitent to your feet."

"And then, my lord," Don Hernando, who had hitherto remained an apparent stranger to all that was taking place, remarked in a mocking voice, "perhaps we are mistaken; do not condemn my brother without hearing him; he is too good a gentleman, and of too old a family, to have committed the faults of which he is accused."

"That is well, Hernando; I am delighted thus to hear you undertake your brother's defence," said the old lady, smiling through her tears, and deceived by his words.

"Certainly, mother; I love my brother too dearly," the young man said, ironically, "to let him be thus accused without proof. That Rodolfo has seduced the daughter of the principal Cacique of the Opatas and made her his mistress is evident, and known to all the world as true, but it is of very little consequence. But what I will never believe until it is proved to me is, that he has married this creature, any more than I will put faith in the calumnies that represent him not only as one of the intimate friends of the Curate Hidalgo, but also as one of his most active and influential partisans in this province. No; a thousand times No! A gentleman of the name and blood of Tobar knows too well what honour demands to commit such infamy! Acting so would be utter apostasy, and complete forgetfulness of all that a noble Castilian owes to himself, his ancestors, and that honour of which he is only the holder. Come, Rodolfo; come, my brother, raise your head: confound the calumniators; give a solemn denial to those who have dared to sully your reputation! One word from you, but one that proves your perfect innocence, and the storm unjustly aroused against you will be dispersed; my father will open his arms to you, and all will be forgotten."

During this speech, whose deep perfidy the Count recognised, he was suffering from extreme emotion. At the first words his brother uttered, he started as if he felt the sting of a viper; but gradually his anger had made way for contempt in his heart; and it was with a smile of crushing disdain that he listened to the emphatic and mocking conclusion.

"Well, my son," the Marquis said, "you see everybody defends you here, while I alone accuse you! What will you answer to prove your innocence to me?"

"Nothing, father!" the young man said, coolly.

"Nothing?" the old gentleman repeated, angrily.

"No, father!" he continued; "because, if I attempted to justify myself, you would not listen to me; and that, supposing you consented to listen to me, you would not comprehend me. Oh! do not mistake my meaning," he said, on seeing the Marquis about to speak; "you would not understand me, father, not through want of intellect, but through pride. Proud of your name and the privileges it gives, you are accustomed to judge men and things from a peculiar point of view, and understand honour in your own fashion."

"Are there two sorts of honour, then?" the Marquis exclaimed, involuntarily.

"No, father," Don Rodolfo answered, calmly, "there is only one; but there are two ways of comprehending it: and my brother, who a moment back told you without incurring your disapproval that a gentleman had the right to abuse the love of a maiden and make her his mistress, but that the honour of his name would forbid him marrying her, seems to me to have studied the point thoroughly, and is better able than I to discuss it. As you said yourself, father, we must come to an end. Well, be it so. I will not attempt to continue an impossible struggle with you. When I received orders to come to you, I knew I was condemned beforehand, and yet I obediently attended your summons; it was because my resolution was irrevocably formed. What am I reproached with? Having married the daughter of an Indian Cacique? It is true; I avow openly that I have done so: her birth is perhaps as good as mine, but most certainly her heart is greater. What is the next charge—that I am a friend of the Curate Hidalgo, and one of his firmest adherents? That is also true; and I am happy and proud of this friendship: I glory in these aspirations for liberty with which you reproach me as a crime. Descendants of the first conquerors of Mexico, this land, discovered and subjugated by our fathers, has become our country; for the last three centuries we have not been Spaniards, but Mexicans. The hour has at length arrived for us to shake off the yoke of this self-called country, which has so long been battening on our blood and tears, and enriching itself with our gold. In speaking thus to you, my venerated father, my heart is broken, for Heaven is my witness that I have a profound respect and love for you. I know that I am invoking on my head all the weight of your anger, and that anger will be terrible! but, in my sorrow, one sublime hope is left to me. Faithful to the motto of our ancestors, I have done everything for honour; my conscience is calm; and some day—soon, perhaps—you will forgive me, for you will see that I have not failed in fealty."

"Never!" the Marquis shouted in a voice the more terrible because the constraint he had been forced to place on himself, in order to hear his son's speech to the end, had been so great. "Begone! I no longer know you! You are no longer my son! Begone!—villain! I give you my——"

"Oh!" the Marchioness shrieked, as she threw herself into his arms, "do not curse him, sir! Do not add that punishment to the one you have inflicted on him. The unhappy boy is already sufficiently punished. No one has the right to curse him; a father less than any other—for in that case it is God who avenges."

The Marquis stood for a moment silent and gloomy, then stretched out his arms to his son, and shook his head sadly.

"Begone!" he said in a hollow voice. "May God watch over you—for henceforth you have no family. Farewell!"

The young man, pale and trembling, bent beneath the weight of this sentence; then rose and tottered out of the room without saying a word.

"My son!—my son!" the Marchioness exclaimed in a heart-rending voice.

The implacable old man quickly stopped her at the moment when, half-mad with grief, she was rushing from the daïs, and pointed to Don Hernando, who was bowing hypocritically to her.

"You have only one son, madam," he said, in a harsh voice, "and that son is here."

The Marchioness uttered a cry of despair, and, crushed with grief, fell senseless at her husband's feet; who, also overcome in this fearful struggle of pride of race against paternal love, sank into a chair and buried his face in his hands, while a mighty sob escaped from his bosom.

Don Hernando had rushed after his brother, not for the purpose of consoling or bringing him back, but solely not to let the joy be seen which covered his face at this mournful scene, all the fearful incidents in which he had been so long preparing with feline patience.

CHAPTER VIII.

THE TWO BROTHERS.

AFTER quitting the Red Room, Don Rodolfo, under the weight of the condemnation pronounced against him, with broken heart and burning head had rushed onwards, flying the paternal anger, and resolved to leave the hacienda as quickly as possible, never to return to it. His horse was still in the first yard, where he had tied it up. The young man went up to it, seized the bridle, and placed his foot in the stirrup. At the same moment a hand was laid on his shoulder—Don Rodolfo turned as if seared with a hot iron. His brother was standing before him.

A feverish redness suffused his face; his hands closed, and his eyes flashed lightning; but at once extinguishing the fire of his glance and affecting a forced calmness, he said, in a firm voice—

"What do you want, brother?"

"To press your hand before your departure, Rodolfo," the young man said, with a whining voice.

Rodolfo looked at him for a moment with an expression of profound disdain, then unhooking the sword that hung at his side, he handed it to his brother.

"There, Hernando," he said, ironically, "it is only right that, since you will henceforth bear the name and honour of our family, this sword should revert to you. You desired my inheritance, and success has crowned your efforts."

"Brother," the young man stammered.

"I am not reproaching you," Don Rodolfo continued, haughtily. "Enjoy in peace those estates you have torn from me. May Heaven grant that the burden may not appear to you some day too heavy, and that the recollection of the deed you have done may not poison your last years. Henceforth we shall never meet again on this earth. Farewell!" And letting the sword he had offered his brother fall on the ground, he leaped on his horse and went off at full speed, without even giving a parting glance at those walls which had seen his birth, and from which he was now eternally banished. Don Hernando stood for a moment with hanging head and pale face, crushed by the shame and consciousness of the bad action he had not feared to commit. Already remorse was beginning to prey on him. At length, when the galloping of the horse had died away in the distance, he raised his eyes, wiped away the perspiration that inundated his face, and picked up the sword lying at his feet.

"Poor Rodolfo!" he muttered, stifling a sigh; "I am very guilty."

And he slowly returned to the hacienda. Count Don Rodolfo de Moguer kept the word he had given his brother: he never reappeared. Nothing was ever heard of him, and his intimate friends never saw him again after his journey to the hacienda, nor knew what had become of him. The next year, a few Indians who escaped from the massacre at the bridge of Calderon, when Hidalgo was defeated by the Spanish General Callega, spread the report that Don Rodolfo, who during the whole action kept by Hidalgo's side, was killed in a desperate charge he made into the heart of the Spanish lines, in the hope of restoring the fortunes of the day; but this rumour was not confirmed. In spite of all the measures taken by the Marquis, the young man's body was not found among the dead, and his fate remained a mystery for the family.

In the meanwhile, Don Hernando, by his father's orders, had succeeded to his brother's title, and almost immediately married Dona Aurelia del Torre Azul, originally destined for Don Rodolfo. The Marquis and Marchioness lived some few years longer. They died a few days after one another, bearing with them a poisoned sting of remorse for having banished their first-born son from their presence.

But, inflexible up to his dying hour, the Marquis never once made a complaint, and died without mentioning his son's name. However, the Marquis's hopes were realized ere he descended to the grave, for he had the supreme consolation of seeing his family continued in his grandchildren.

At the funeral, a man was noticed in the crowd wrapped up in a wide cloak, and his features concealed by the broad brim of his hat being pulled over them. No one was able to say who this man was, although one old servant declared he had recognised Don Rodolfo. Was it really the banished son who had come for the last time to pay homage to his father and weep on his tomb? The arrival of the stranger was so unexpected, and his departure so sudden, that it was impossible to get at the truth of the statement.

Then, time passed away, important events succeeded each other, and Don Rodolfo, of whom nothing was heard, was considered dead by his family and friends, and then forgotten; and Don Hernando inherited without dispute the title and estates.

The Marquis de Moguer, in spite of the light under which we have shown him to our readers, was not a wicked man, as might be supposed; but as a younger son, with no other hope than the tonsure, devoured by ambition, and freely enjoying life, he internally rebelled against the harsh and unjust law which exiled him from the pleasures of the world and condemned him to the solitude of the cloister. Assuredly, had his brother frankly accepted his position as first-born, and consented to undertake its duties, Don Hernando would never have thought for a moment of defrauding him of his rights. But when he saw Don Rodolfo despise the old tradition of his race—forget what he owed to his honour as a gentleman, so far as to marry an Indian girl and make common cause with the partisans of the Revolution, he eagerly seized the opportunity chance so providentially offered him to seize the power lost by his brother, and quietly put himself in his place. He thought that, in acting thus, he was not committing a bad action, but almost asserting a right by substituting himself for a man who seemed to care very little for titles and fortune.

Don Hernando, while whitewashing himself in this way, only obeyed that law of justice and injustice which God has placed in the heart of man, and which impels him, when he does any dishonourable deed, to seek excuses in order to prove to himself that he was bound to act as he had done. Still, the Marquis did not dare confess to himself that the chance by which he profited he had helped by all his power, by envenoming by his speeches and continual insinuations his brother's actions, ruining him gradually in his father's mind, and preparing, long beforehand, the condemnation eventually uttered in the Red Room against the unfortunate Rodolfo.

And yet, strange contradiction of the human heart, Don Hernando dearly loved his brother; he pitied him—he would have liked to hold him back on the verge of the precipice down which he thrust him, as it were. Once master of the estates and head of the family, he would have liked to find his brother again, in order to share with him this badly-acquired fortune, and gain pardon for his usurpation.

Unfortunately, these reflections came too late—Don Rodolfo had disappeared without leaving a trace, and hence the Marquis was compelled to restrict himself to sterile regrets. At times, tortured by the ever-present memory of the last scene at the hacienda, he asked himself whether it would not have been better for him to have had a frank explanation with his brother, after which Don Rodolfo, whose simple tastes agreed but badly with the exigencies of a great name, would have amicably renounced in his favour the rights which his position as elder brother gave him.

But now to continue our narrative, which we have too long interrupted.

At the beginning of 1822, on a day of madness which was to be expiated by years of disaster, the definitive separation took place between Spain and Mexico, and the era of *pronunciamentos* set in. After the ephemeral reign of the Emperor Iturbide, Mexico reverted to a republic, or, more correctly, to a military government. Under the pressure of an army of 20,000 soldiers, which had 24,000 officers, the Presidents succeeded each other with headlong speed, burying the nation deeper and deeper in the mire, in which it is now struggling, and which will eventually swallow it up.

By *pronunciamento* on *pronunciamento* Mexico had reached the period when this story begins; but her wealth had been swallowed up in the tornado—her commerce was annihilated, her cities were falling in ruins, and New Spain had only retained of her old splendours fugitive recollections and piles of ruins. The Spaniards had suffered greatly during the War of Independence, as had their partisans, whose property had been burned and plundered by the revolutionists. The fatal decree of 1827, pronouncing the expulsion of the Spaniards, dealt the final and most terrible blow to their fortunes.

The Marquis de Moguer was one of the persons most affected by this measure, although, during the entire War of Independence and the different governments that succeeded each other, he had taken the greatest care not to mix himself up at all in politics, and remained neutral between all parties. This position, which it was difficult and almost impossible to maintain for any length of time, had compelled him to make concessions painful to his pride: unfortunately, his fortune consisted of land and mines, and if he left Mexico he would be a ruined man.

His friends advised him frankly to join the Mexican government, and give up his Spanish nationality. The Marquis, forced by circumstances, followed their advice; and, thanks to the credit some persons enjoyed with the President of the Republic, Don Hernando was not only not disturbed, but authorized to remain in the country, where he was naturalized as a Mexican.

But things had greatly changed with the Marquis. His immense fortune had vanished with the Spanish government. During the ten years of the War of Independence, his estates had lain fallow, and his mines, deserted by the workmen he formerly employed, had gradually become filled with water. They could not be put in working order again except by enormous and most expensive works. The situation was critical, especially for a man reared in luxury and accustomed to sow his money broadcast. He was now compelled to calculate every outlay with the utmost care, if he did not wish to see the hideous spectre of want rise implacable before him.

The pride of the Marquis was broken in this struggle against poverty; his love for his children restored his failing courage, and he bravely resolved to make head against the storm. Like the ruined gentlemen who tilled the soil, with their sword by their side, as a proof of their nobility, he openly became haciendero and miner,—that is to say, he cultivated his estates on a large scale, and bred cattle and horses, while trying to pump out the water which had taken possession of his mines. Unfortunately, he was deficient in two important things for the proper execution of his plans: the necessary knowledge to assist the different operations he meditated; and, above all, money, without which nothing was possible. The Marquis was therefore compelled to engage a majordomo, and borrow on mortgage. For the first few years all went well, or appeared to do so. The majordomo, Don José Paredes, to whom we shall have occasion to refer more fully hereafter, was one of those men so valuable in haciendas, whose life is spent on horseback, whose attention nothing escapes, who thoroughly understand the cultivation of the soil, and know what it ought to produce, almost to an arroba.

But if the estates of the Marquis were beginning to regain their value under the skilful direction of the bailiff, it was not the same with the mines. Taking advantage of the convulsions in which Mexico was writhing, the independent Indians, no longer held in subjection by a fear of the powerful military organization of the Spaniards, had crossed the frontiers and regained a certain portion of their territory. They had permanently settled upon it, and would not allow white men to encroach on it. Most of the Marquis's mines being situated in the very country now occupied by the Indians, were consequently lost to him. The others, almost entirely inundated, in spite of the incessant labour bestowed on them, did not yet hold out any hopes of becoming productive again.

What Don Hernando gained on one side he lost on the other; and his position, in spite of his efforts, became worse and worse, and the abyss of debt gradually enlarged. The Marquis saw with terror the moment before him when it would be impossible for him to continue the struggle. Sad and aged by sorrow rather than years, the Marquis no longer dared to regard the future, which daily became more gloomy for him. He watched in mournful resignation the downfall of his house—the decay of his race; seeking in vain, like the man without a compass on the mighty ocean, from what point of the horizon the vessel that would save him from shipwreck would arrive.

But, alas! days succeeded days without bringing any other change in the position of the Marquis, save greater poverty, and more nearly impending ruin. In proportion as the misfortune came nearer, the Marquis had seen his relations and friends keep aloof from him; all abandoned him, with that selfish indifference which seems a fundamental law of every organized society, when the precept, "Each man for himself," is put in practice, with all the brutal force of the *væ victis*.

Hence Don Hernando resided alone, with his son, at the Hacienda del Toro; for he had lost his wife several years before, and his daughter was being educated in a convent at the town of Rosario; with that noble pride which so admirably becomes men of well-tempered minds, the Marquis had accepted without a murmur the ostracism passed upon him. Far from indulging in useless recriminations with men, the majority of whom had, in other days, received obligations from him, he had made his son a partner in his labours, and, aided by him, redoubled his efforts and his courage.

Some months before the period when our story begins, ill-fortune had seemed, not to grow weary of persecuting the Marquis, but desirous of granting him a truce—this is how a gleam of sunshine penetrated the gloomy atmosphere of the hacienda. One morning, a stranger, who appeared to have come a great distance, stopped at the gate, leading a mule loaded with two bales. This man, on reaching the first courtyard, threw the mule's bridle to a peon, with the simple remark,—

"For Senor Don Hernando de Moguer—"

and, without awaiting an answer, he started down the rocky road at a gallop, and was lost in the windings of the path ere the peon had recovered from the surprise caused by the strange visit. The Marquis, at once warned, had the mule unloaded, and the bales conveyed to his study. They each contained twenty-five thousand piastres in gold, or nearly eleven thousand pounds of our money: on a folded paper was written one word—Restitution.

It was in vain that the Marquis ordered the most minute researches; the strange messenger could not be found. Don Hernando was therefore compelled to keep this large sum, which arrived so opportunely to extricate him from a difficult position, for he had a considerable payment to make on the morrow. Still, it was only on the repeated assurances of Don Ruiz and the majordomo, that the money was really his, that he consented to use it.

Cheered by this change of fortune, Don

Hernando at length consented that Don Ruiz should go and fetch his sister, and bring her back to the hacienda, where her presence had been long desired; though there had been an obstacle, in the dangers of such a journey.

We will now resume our narrative, begging the reader to forgive this long digression, which was indispensable for the due comprehension of what is about to follow, and lead him to the Hacienda del Toro, a few hours before the arrival of Don Ruiz and his sister; that is to say, about three weeks since we left them at the post of San Miguel.

CHAPTER IX.

A NEW CHARACTER.

ALTHOUGH, owing to its position on the shores of the Pacific, Sonora enjoys the blessings of the sea breeze, whose moisture at intervals refreshes the heated atmosphere; still, for three hours in the afternoon, the earth incessantly heated by the torrid sunbeams produces a crushing heat. At such times the country assumes a really desolate aspect beneath the cloudless sky, which seems an immense plate of red-hot iron. The birds suddenly cease their songs, and languidly hide themselves beneath the thick foliage of the trees, which bow their proud crests towards the ground. Men and domestic animals hasten to seek shelter in the houses, raising in their hurried progress a white, impalpable, and calcined dust, which enters mouth and nostrils. For some hours Sonora is converted into a vast desert from which every appearance of life and movement has disappeared.

Everybody is asleep, or at least reclining in the most shady rooms, with closed eyes, and with the body abandoned to that species of somnolency which is neither sleeping nor waking, and which from that very fact is filled with such sweet and voluptuous reveries—inhaling at deep draughts the artificial breeze produced by artfully-contrived currents of air, and in a word indulging in what is generally called in the torrid zones a siesta.

These are hours full of enjoyment, of whose sweet and beneficent influence on body and mind we busy, active Englishmen are ignorant, but which people nearer the sun revel in. The Italians call this state the *dolce far niente*, and the Turks, that essentially sensual race, *keff*.

Like that city in the "Arabian Nights," the inhabitants of which the wicked enchanter suddenly changed into statues by waving his wand, life seemed suddenly arrested at the Hacienda del Toro, for the silence was so profound: peons, vaqueros, criados, everybody in fact, were enjoying their siesta. It was about three in the afternoon; but that indistinct though significant buzz, which announces the awakening of the hour that precedes the resumption of labour was audible. Two gentlemen alone had not yielded to sleep, in spite of the crushing midday heat; but seated in an elegantly-furnished *cuarto*, they had spent the hours usually devoted to slumber in conversation. The cause for this deviation from the ordinary custom must have been most serious. The Hispano-American and especially the Mexican does not lightly sacrifice those hours of repose during which, according to a Spanish proverb, only dogs and Frenchmen are to be seen in the sun.

Of these two gentlemen, one, Don Hernando de Moguer, is already known to us. Years, while stooping his back, had furrowed some wrinkles on his forehead, and mingled many silver threads with his hair; but the expression of his face, with the exception of a tinge of melancholy spread over his features by lengthened misfortunes, had remained nearly the same, that is to say, gentle and timid, although clever; slightly sarcastic and eminently crafty.

As for the person with whom Don Hernando was conversing at this moment, he deserves a detailed description, physically at least, for the reader will soon be enabled to appreciate his moral character. He was a short plump man, with a rubicund face and apoplectic look, though hardly forty years of age. Still his hair, which was almost white, his deeply wrinkled forehead, and his grey eyes buried beneath bushy whiskers, gave him a senile appearance, harmonizing but little with the sharp gesticulation and youthful manner he affected. His long, thin, violet nose was bent like a parrot's beak over a wide mouth filled with dazzling white teeth; and his prominent cheekbones, covered with blue veins, completed a strange countenance, the expression of which bore a striking likeness to that of an owl.

This species of nutcracker, with his prominent stomach and short ill-hung limbs, whose whole appearance was most disagreeable, had such a mobility of face as rendered it impossible to read his thoughts on his features, in the event of this fat man's carcase containing a thought. His cold blue eyes were ever pertinaciously fixed on the person addressing him, and did not reveal the slightest emotion; in short, this man produced at the first contact that invariable antipathy which is felt on the approach of reptiles, and which, after nearer acquaintance, is converted into disgust and contempt.

He was a certain Don Rufino Contreras, one of the richest landowners in Sonora, and a year previously had been elected senator to the Mexican Congress for the province.

At the moment when we enter the *cuarto*, Don Hernando, with arms folded at his back and frowning brow, is walking up and down, while Don Rufino, seated on a *butacca*, with his body thrown back, is following his movements with a crafty smile on his lips, while striving to scratch off an invisible spot on his knee. For some minutes, the haciendero continued his walk, and then stopped before Don Rufino, who bent on him a mocking, inquiring glance.

"Then," he said, in a voice whose anxious expression he sought in vain to conceal, "you must positively have the entire sum within a week?"

"Yes," the fat man replied, still smiling.

"Why, if that is the case, did you not warn me sooner?"

"It was through delicacy, my dear sir."

"What—through delicacy?" Don Hernando repeated, with a start of surprise.

".You shall judge for yourself."

"I shall be glad to do so."

"I believe you do me the justice of allowing that I am your friend?"

"You have said you are, at least."

"I fancy I have proved it to you."

"No matter; but let us pass over that."

"Very well. Knowing that you were in a critical position at the moment, I tried to procure the sum by all possible means, as I did not wish to have recourse to you, except in the last extremity. You see, my dear Don Hernando, how delicate and truly friendly my calculations were. Unfortunately, at the present time it is very difficult to get money in, owing to the stagnation of trade produced by the new conflict which threatens to break out between the President of the Republic and the Southern States. It was therefore literally impossible for me to obtain the smallest sum. In such a perplexing position, I leave you to judge what I was obliged to do. The money I must have; you have owed it for a long time, and I applied to you—what else could I do?"

"I do not know. Still, I think you might have sent a peon to warn me, before you left Sonora."

"No, my dear sir, that is exactly what I should not do. I have not come direct to you: in pursuance of the line of conduct I laid down I hoped to collect the required sum on my road, and not be obliged to come all the way to your hacienda."

Don Hernando made no reply. He began his walk again after giving the speaker a glance which would have given him cause for thought, had he noticed it; but the latter gentleman had begun rubbing the invisible spot again with more obstinacy than before. In the meanwhile the sunbeams had become more and more oblique; the hacienda had woke up to its ordinary life; outside the shouts of the vaqueros pricking the oxen or urging on the horses could be heard mingled with the lowing and neighing of the draught-cattle. Don Hernando walked up to a window the shutters of which he threw open, and a refreshing breeze entered the *cuarto*. Don Rufino gave a sigh of relief and sat up in his *butacca*.

"Ouf," he said, with an expression of comfort, "I was very tired; not through the long ride I was compelled to make this morning, so much as through the stifling heat."

Don Hernando started at this insinuation, as if he had been stung by a serpent; he had neglected all the laws of Mexican hospitality; for Don Rufino's visit had so disagreeably surprised him, and made him forget all else before the sudden obligation of satisfying the claims of a merciless creditor. But at Don Rufino's remarks he understood how unusual his conduct must have seemed to a weary traveller, hence he rang a bell, and a peon at once came in.

"Refreshment," he said.

The peon bowed, and left the room.

"You will excuse me, Caballero," the haciendero continued, frankly, "but your visit so surprised me, that at the moment I did not think of offering the refreshment which a tired traveller requires so much. Your room is prepared, rest yourself to-night, and to-morrow we will resume our conversation, and arrive at a solution I trust mutually satisfactory."

"I hope so, my dear sir. Heaven is my witness that it is my greatest desire," Don Rufino answered, as he raised to his lips the glass of orangeade brought by the peon. "Unhappily I fear that, with the best will in the world, we cannot come to a settlement unless——"

"Unless!" Don Hernando sharply interrupted. Don Rufino quietly sipped his orangeade, placed the glass on the table, and said, as he threw himself back on the *butacca*, and rolled a cigarette—

"Unless you pay me in full what you owe me, which, from what you have said, appears to me to be difficult, I confess."

"Ah!" Don Hernando remarked with an air of constraint, "what makes you suppose that?"

"I beg your pardon, my dear sir, I suppose nothing: you told me just now that you were hardly pressed."

"Well, and what conclusion do you derive from that?" the haciendero asked impatiently.

"A very simple thing—that seventy thousand piastres form a rather round sum, and that however rich a man may be, he does not always have it in his hands, especially when he is pressed."

"I can make sacrifices."

"Believe me, I shall be sincerely sorry."

"But can you not wait a few days longer?"

"Impossible, I repeat; let us understand our respective positions, in order to avoid any business misunderstanding, which should always be prevented between honourable gentlemen holding a certain position. I lent you that sum, and only stipulated for small interest, I believe."

"I allow it, Senor, and thank you for it."

"It is not really worth the trouble; I was anxions to oblige you. I did so, and let us say no more about it; but remember that I made one condition which you accepted."

"Yes," Don Hernando said, with an impatient start, "and I was wrong."

"Perhaps so; but that is not the question. This condition which you accepted was to the effect that you should repay me the sum I advanced upon demand."

"Have I said the contrary?"

"Far from it; but now that I want the money, I ask you for it, and that is natural: I have in no way infringed the conditions. You ought to have expected what is happening to-day, and taken your precautions accordingly."

"Hence, if I ask a month to collect the money you claim?"

"I should be heart-broken, but should refuse; for I want the money, not in a month but in a week. I can quite put myself in your position, and comprehend how disagreeable the matter must be: but unluckily so it is."

What most hurt Don Hernando was not the recal of the loan, painful as it was to him, so much as the way in which the demand was made; the show of false good-nature employed by his creditor, and the insulting pity he displayed. Carried away involuntarily by the rage that filled his heart, he was about to give Don Rufino an answer which would have broken off all friendly relations between them for ever, when a great noise was heard in the hacienda, mingled with shouts of joy and the stamping of horses. Don Hernando eagerly leant out of the window, and at the expiration of a moment, turned round to Don Rufino, who was sucking his cigarette with an air of beatitude.

"Here are my children, Caballero," he said; "not a word of this affair before them, I entreat."

"I know too well what I owe you, my dear Senor," the other replied, as he prepared to rise. "With your permission, however, I will withdraw, in order to allow you entire liberty for your family joy."

"No, no!" Don Hernando added, "I had better introduce you at once to my son and daughter."

"As you please, my dear sir. I shall be flattered to form the acquaintance of your charming family."

The door opened, and Don José Paredes appeared. The majordomo was a half-breed of about forty years of age, tall and powerfully built, with bow legs and round shoulders that denoted his capacity as a horseman; in fact, the worthy man's life was spent in the saddle, galloping about the country. He took a side glance at Don Rufino, bowed to his master, and lowering his usual rough tone, said—

"Senor amo, the nino and nina have arrived in good health, thanks to Our Lady of Carnero."

"Thanks, Don José," Don Hernando replied; "let them come in. I shall be delighted to see them."

The majordomo gave a signal outside, and the two young people rushed into the room. With one bound they were in their father's arms, who for a moment pressed them to his heart; but then he pushed them away, remarking that a stranger was present. The young couple bowed respectfully.

"Senor Don Rufino," the Marquis said, "I present to you my son, Don Ruiz de Moguer, and my daughter, Donna Marianita: my children, this is Senor Don Rufino Contreras, one of my best friends."

"A title of which I am proud," Don Rufino replied, with a bow, while giving the young lady a cold searching glance, which made her look down involuntarily and blush.

"Are the apartments ready, Don José?" Don Hernando continued.

"Yes, excellency," the majordomo said, who was contemplating the young people with a radiant face.

"If Senor Don Rufino will permit it, you can go and lie down, my children," the haciendero said. "You must be tired."

"You will also allow me to rest, Don Hernando?" the Senator then said. The haciendero bowed.

"We will resume our conversation at a more favourable moment," he continued, as he took a side-glance at Donna Marianita, who was just leaving the room with her brother. "However, my dear Senor, do not feel too anxious about my visit; for I believe I have discovered a way of arranging matters without inconveniencing you too much."

And, bowing to his knees to the Marquis, who was astounded at this conduct, which he was so far from expecting, Don Rufino left the room, smiling with an air of protection.

CHAPTER X.

DON JOSÉ PAREDES.

Several days had elapsed since the return of Don Ruiz and his sister to the hacienda, and Don Rufino had not said a word about the money which occasioned his visit. The haciendero, while employing all the means in his power to procure the necessary sum to pay his debt, had been careful not to allude to the conversation he had held with his creditor on the first day; the more so because Don Rufino seemed to have forgotten the pressing want of money he had at first given as his excuse for not granting any delay.

At the hacienda everything had returned to its old condition. Don Ruiz went out on horseback in the morning with José Paredes, in order to watch the peons and vaqueros, leaving to his father and sister the care of doing the honours to Don Rufino. For the first two or three days Donna Marianita had been considerably embarrassed by their guest's obsequious smiles and passionate glances; but she soon made up her mind, and only laughed at the craving look and absurd postures of the stout gentleman. The latter, while perceiving the effect he produced on the young lady, appeared to take no heed of it, and conscientiously continued his manœuvres with the tenacity that formed the basis of his character. Probably in acting thus, and by openly paying his court to Donna Marianita, in the presence of her father and brother, Don Rufino was carrying out a pre-arranged plan, in order to gain an end which may be easily guessed.

It was evident to everybody that Don Rufino was seeking to obtain the hand of Donna Marianita. Don Hernando, in spite of the secret annoyance this pursuit caused him, for this man was the last he would have desired as his son-in-law, did not dare, however, let his vexation be seen, owing to his delicate position, and the sword of Damocles which Don Rufino held in suspense over his head. He contented himself with watching him closely, while leaving him free to act, hoping everything from him, and striving to collect all his resources in order to pay him off as speedily as possible; and once liberty was regained, to dismiss him. Unfortunately, money was difficult to obtain. Most of Don Hernando's debtors failed in meeting their engagements; and it was with great difficulty he obtained at the end of a fortnight one quarter the sum he owed Don Rufino, and this sum even could not be employed in liquidating the debt, for it was indispensable for the continuation of the works at the hacienda.

Since his arrival at the hacienda, Don Rufino had sent off messengers in several directions, and received letters. One morning he entered Don Hernando's study with an easy air, where the latter passed nearly the day, engaged in the most abstruse calculations. The haciendero raised his head with amazement on seeing the Senator; it was the first time the latter had come to seek him in this room. He suffered a heart-pang; but he succeeded in hiding his emotion, and good-humouredly invited his visitor to take a seat.

"My dear Senor," Don Rufino began, as he comfortably stretched himself out upon a *butacca,* "excuse me for pursuing you into your last entrenchments, but I want to talk seriously with you, and so I frankly knocked at this door."

"You have done well," Don Hernando answered, with ill-dissembled agony: "you know that I am entirely at your disposal. How can I be of any service to you?"

"I will not trouble you long: I am not fond of lengthy conversations, and have merely come to terminate the affair which we began on the day when I arrived at the hacienda."

The haciendero felt a cold perspiration stand on his temples at this brutally frank avowal.

"I had not forgotten you," he replied: "at this very moment I am making arrangements which, I trust, will enable me to discharge the debt in a few days."

"That is not the point," Don Rufino remarked, airily: "I do not want the money, and request you to hold it for me as long as you possibly can."

Don Hernando looked at him in amazement. "That surprises you," the Senator continued, "and yet the affair is very simple. I was anxious to prove to you that you had in me not a pressing creditor, but a truly devoted friend. When I saw that it would greatly embarrass you to repay me this trifle, and as you are a gentleman I am anxious to oblige, I turned to another quarter."

"Still," Don Hernando, who feared a snare, objected: "you said to me——"

"I believed it," Don Rufino interrupted him. "Fortunately it was not so, as I have recently acquired the proof: not only have I been able to meet my payment, but I have a considerable sum left in my hands which I do not know what to do with, and which I should feel much obliged by your taking; for I do not know a more honourable gentleman than yourself, and I wish to get rid of the money, which is useless to me at the moment."

Don Hernando, confounded by this overture, which he had been so far from expecting from a man who had at first been so harsh with him, was silent, for he knew not what to answer, or to what he should attribute this so sudden and extraordinary change.

"Good gracious!" continued Don Rufino, with a smile; "during the few days I have been with you, my dear Senor, I have been enabled to appreciate the intelligent way in which you manage your immense estate; and it is evident to me that you must realize enormous profits. Unfortunately for you, you are in the position of all men who undertake great things with limited resources. You are short of capital just at the moment when it is most necessary; but as this is a common case, you cannot complain. You have made sacrifices, and will have to make more before obtaining real results. The money you want I have, and I offer it to you. I trust you will not insult me by doubting my friendship, or my desire to be of service to you."

"Certainly, Caballero. Still," Don Hernando stammered, "I am already your debtor to a heavy amount."

"Well, what matter? You will be my debtor for a larger amount, that is all."

"I understand all the delicacy and kindness of your conduct, but I fear——"

"What?—that I may demand repayment at an inconvenient moment?"

"I will not conceal from you——"

"You are wrong, Don Hernando. I wish to deal with you as a friend, and do you a real service. You owe me seventy thousand piastres, I believe?"

"Alas, yes!"

"Why that 'alas?'" the senator asked, with a smile. "Seventy thousand piastres, and fifty thousand more I am going to hand you directly, in six bills payable at sight, drawn on Wilson and Co., Bankers, at Hermosillo, will form a round sum, for which you will give me your acceptance payable—come, what date will suit you best?"

Don Hernando hesitated. Evidently Don Rufino, in making him so strange a proposal, had an object; but that object he could not see. The Senator's love for his daughter could not impel him to do such a generous act: this unexpected kindness evidently concealed a snare; but what was the snare? Don Rufino carefully followed the different feelings that were reflected on Don Hernando's face.

"You hesitate," he said to him, "and you are wrong. Let us talk candidly. You cannot possibly hope to realize any profit within eight months, so it will be impossible for you to pay me so large a sum before that period." Then, opening his pocket-book and taking out the six bills, which he laid on the table, he continued: "Here are the fifty thousand piastres; give me an acceptance for one hundred and twenty thousand, payable at twelve months' date. You see that I give you all necessary latitude to turn yourself round. Well, supposing — which is not probable — that you are unable to pay me when the bill falls due; we will renew it, that is all. *Cuerpo de Cristo!* I am not a harsh creditor. Come, is the matter settled, or must I take the bills back?"

Money, under whatever shape it presents itself, has an irresistible attraction in the eyes of the speculator and embarrassed man. Don Hernando, in spite of all his efforts— in spite of all the numerous sacrifices he had made, felt himself rapidly going down the incline of ruin, on which it is impossible for a man to stop; but time might save him. Don Rufino, whatever his wishes might be, rendered him an immense service by giving him, not only time, but also the money he required, and which he despaired of obtaining elsewhere. Any longer hesitation on his part would therefore have been unjustifiable; hence he took the bills, and gave his acceptance.

"That's settled," Don Rufino said, as he

folded the document and carefully placed it in his pocket-book. "My dear Senor, you are really a singular man. There is more difficulty in getting you to accept money than there would be in getting another to pay it."

"I really do not know how to thank you, Don Rufino, for the service you have rendered me, and which I am now free to confess has arrived very opportunely."

"Money is always opportune," the Senator replied, with a laugh; "but let us say no more about that. If you happen to have a safe man, send him off at once to cash these bills at Hermosillo, for money is too scarce to be allowed to lie idle."

"This very day my majordomo, Don José Paredes, shall set out for the *ciudad*."

"Very good. Now I have one request to make of you."

"Speak, speak! I shall be delighted to prove to you how grateful I am."

"This is the matter: now that I am, temporarily at least, no longer your creditor, I have no decent pretext for remaining at the hacienda."

"Well, what does that matter?"

"It matters a great deal to me. I should like to remain here a few days longer, in order to enjoy your agreeable society."

"Are you jesting, Don Rufino? The longer you remain at the hacienda, the greater honour you will do us; we shall be delighted to keep you, not for a few days, but for all the time you may be pleased to grant us."

"Very good; that is what I desired. Now, I shall go away and leave you to your business."

When the majordomo returned to the hacienda at about eleven o'clock in the morning, Don Hernando sent for him. Without taking the time to pull off his vaquera boots or unbuckle his heavy spurs, José Paredes hurried to his master.

"Have you a good horse?" the haciendero asked, so soon as the majordomo entered the study.

"I have several, Excellency," he answered.

"I mean by a good horse, one capable of going a long distance."

"Certainly, mi amo; I have a mustang on which I could ride to Hermosillo and back without giving it any further rest than that of the camping hours."

"I want to send you to Hermosillo."

"Very good, Excellency; when must I start?"

"Why, as soon as possible after you have rested."

"Rested from what?"

"The ride you have taken this morning."

The majordomo shrugged his shoulders with a smile.

"I am never tired, Excellency; in half an hour I shall have lassoed my horse, saddled it, and mounted, unless you wish me to defer my journey."

"The hours for the siesta will soon be here, and the heat will be insufferable."

"You are aware, Excellency, that we half-Indians are children of the sun; its heat does not affect us."

"You have an answer for everything, Don José."

"For you, Excellency, I feel myself capable of performing impossibilities."

"I know that you are devoted to my house."

"Is it not just, Excellency? For two

centuries my family has eaten the bread of yours; and, if I acted otherwise than I am doing, I should be unworthy of those from whom I am descended."

"I thank you, my friend; you know the esteem and affection I have for you. I am about to intrust an important commission to you."

"Be assured that I shall perform it, Excellency."

"Very good. You will start at once for Hermosillo, where you will cash these bills for fifty thousand piastres, at the bank of Wilson and Co."

"Fifty thousand piastres!" the major-domo repeated, with surprise.

"It surprises you, my friend, to whom I have confided my most secret affairs, that I have so large a sum to receive. You ask yourself, doubtless, in what way I managed to obtain it."

"I ask nothing, Excellency; it does not concern me. I am here to carry out your orders, and not permit myself improper observations."

"This money has been lent me by a friend whose kindness is inexhaustible."

"Heaven grant that you are not mistaken, Excellency; and that the man from whom you have this money is really a friend."

"What do you mean, Don José? To what are you alluding?"

"I make no allusion, mi amo; I merely think that friends who lend fifty thousand piastres from hand to hand—pardon my frankness, Excellency—to a man whose affairs are in such a condition as yours, are very rare at present; and that, before forming a definite judgment about them, it would be wiser to wait and learn the cause of such singular generosity."

Don Hernando sighed. He shared his majordomo's opinions, though he would not allow it. Following the tactics of all men who have not good reasons to allege, he suddenly turned the conversation.

"You can take three or four persons with you," he said.

"What to do, Excellency?"

"Why, to act as escort on your return."

The majordomo began laughing.

"What use is an escort, Excellency? You want your money here? I will buy a mule at Hermosillo, and load the money on it, and it will take a very clever fellow to rob me, I assure you."

"Still, it would be, perhaps, better to have an escort."

"Permit me to remark, Excellency, that it would be the best way of setting robbers on my track."

"*Viva Dios!* I should be curious to know how you arrive at that conclusion."

"You will easily understand me, mi amo. A single man is certain to pass unnoticed, especially when, as at this moment, the roads are infested with bandits of every description and every colour."

"Hum! what you are saying is not reassuring, Don José, do you know that?" Don Hernando remarked, with a smile, for his majordomo's reasoning amused him.

"On the contrary, the bandits to whom I am referring, Excellency, are clever, too clever, and it is that which ruins them; they will never imagine that a poor devil of a half-breed, leading a sorry mule, can be carrying fifty thousand piastres. Deceived by my appearance, they will let me pass, without even pretending to see; while if I take persons with me, it will arouse their suspicions, they will want to know why I am guarded, and I shall be plundered."

"You may really be right, Don José."

"I am certain I am, Excellency."

"Well, I will not argue any longer; do what you think proper."

"All right, Excellency; I will deliver the money to you, without the loss of a real, I promise you."

"May Heaven grant it: here are the bills, and now—you can start whenever you please."

"I shall be gone within an hour, Excellency," the majordomo answered.

He took up the bills, hid them in his bosom, and, after bowing to his master, left the study. José Paredes went straight to the corral, where in a few minutes he had lassoed a mustang with small head and flashing eye, which he began saddling, after he had carefully rubbed it down. Then he inspected his weapons, laid in a stock of powder and ball, placed some provisions in his alforjas, and mounted. But, instead of leaving the hacienda, he proceeded to a separate building, and twice gently tapped a window before which he pulled up. The window opened, and Don Ruiz appeared.

"Ah! is that you, Paredes; going back to the plantations already?" he said; "well, wait a minute, and I will be with you."

The majordomo shook his head.

"Do not disturb yourself, Nino," he said. "I am not going to the plantations, but on a journey."

"A journey?" the young man asked, in surprise.

"Yes; but only for a few days. The Marquis has sent me, and I shall soon be back."

"Can you tell me the reason why you are going, and whither?"

"The master will tell you himself, Nino."

"Good! but I suppose you have some other motive for coming to wish me good-bye?"

"Yes, Nino; I wished to give you a piece of advice before leaving the hacienda."

"Advice!"

"Yes; and of a serious nature. Nino, during my absence, watch carefully the man who is here!"

"Whom do you mean, Paredes?"

"The Senator, Don Rufino Contreras."

"For what reason?"

"Watch him, Nino, watch him! And now, good-bye for the present."

And without awaiting the question the young man was about to ask him, the majordomo dug his spurs into his horse's flanks, and left the hacienda at a gallop.

CHAPTER XI.

ON THE ROAD.

MEXICO, considering its size, is one of the least populated countries in the world. With but few exceptions, the old Spanish colonies, since they have proclaimed their independence and become free republics, having been constantly engaged in war with each other, or in overthrowing the government they themselves elected, have seen all the ties attaching families to the soil broken in turn. Foreigners, no longer finding the necessary safety for their speculations in countries incessantly troubled by revolutions, have gone away. Trade has been annihilated; commerce has fallen into a state of atrophy; and the population has frightfully decreased, with such rapidity that sensible men, who sought a remedy for this incurable evil, called emigration to the help of these states, which nothing can galvanize, and which only possess a factitious existence,

Unfortunately, the Hispano-American race is essentially haughty and jealous. Poor fellows, who let themselves be seduced by the brilliant promises made them, and who consented to cross the sea to settle in this country, found on their arrival, and especially in Mexico, an ill-disguised hatred and contempt, which was displayed in all classes of society by ill-will and aversion. Hence, being disgusted by their reception, and recognising the slight trust they could place in the promises of the men who had summoned them, they hastened to leave a country in which they had only found unjust prejudices and deplorable ill faith, and went to ask of the United States the protection refused them by those who had so pressingly summoned them.

Mexico, in spite of a certain varnish of civilization, the last reminiscence of the Spanish occupation, which may still be found in the large cities and their environs, is, therefore, in reality plunged into a state of barbarism relatively greater than it was fifty years ago. The Pacific States, especially, being less frequently visited by strangers, and left, as it were, to themselves, have retained a peculiar physiognomy, whose picturesque savageness and rough manners would cause the tourist's heart to beat with joy, if ever a tourist ventured into these countries; but which inspire an involuntary fear, justified, however, by everything the traveller, forced to visit this land on business, witnesses.

In Europe and all civilized countries, the means of transport are numerous and convenient, but in Mexico only one is known—the horse. In the Central States, and those which run along the Atlantic seaboard, some towns possess diligences, which change horses at the *tambos*, a species of inn, where the travellers stop to pass the night. But these *tambos* and *mesons*, which possess a great resemblance to the Sicilian hostelries and Spanish ventas, supply absolutely nothing to the guests they shelter, excepting a roof, reduced to its simplest expression; that is to say, the traveller is compelled to take his bed with him, in addition to provisions, if he does not wish to sleep wrapped up in his cloak.

In spite of the numberless disagreements

which the uncomfortable mode of progressing from one place to another entails, the traveller derives one advantage from it—that of not being exposed, in a fickle atmosphere like that of Mexico, where after burning days the nights are chilly, to the attacks of the climate. In the Pacific States, matters are no longer thus; the traveller who proceeds from one town to another is forced to do so on horseback, without any hope of finding for a distance of sixty or eighty leagues the smallest inn, or even most wretched rancho, where he can shelter himself from wind and rain at nightfall. At sunset he camps where he is in the open air, and begins his journey again on the morrow. Still, as Providence has been in its wisdom careful to give an equal amount of good and evil, the robbers, salteadors, and brigands of every description, who infest all the roads in the interior, on which they reign as masters, plundering travellers in open day and assassinating them with the most perfect impunity, are rarely found in Sonora. In this country the roads in this respect enjoy a relatively complete security, except when the Indians have risen, or a fresh *pronunciamento* has let bands of revolted soldiers loose on the country. These fellows have no scruple about imitating professional robbers, and killing and plundering people, whose unlucky stars have exposed them to their tender mercies.

José Paredes, though he had in reality only fifty leagues to go, a distance which in most European countries is comfortably performed in a railway carriage in a few hours, was obliged, on account of the bad state of the roads, and the indispensable precautions he had to take, to remain at least four days on the road before reaching Hermosillo. This journey, which would have been very painful to any man accustomed to the ease and luxuries of life, was only a pleasure-trip for the worthy majordomo, a real Centaur, whose life was spent on horseback—who slept more frequently in the open air than under a roof, and whose powerful constitution rendered him insensible to the annoyances inseparable from a journey made under such conditions. The Mexicans have two expressions which admirably depict the class of men to whom the majordomo belonged; they call them *Ginetes* and *Hombres de a Caballo*.

José Paredes, then, rode along jauntily on

his horse, at one moment carelessly smoking a husk cigarette, at another humming a *jarabe* or a *seguedilla*, while keeping his eye and ear on the watch, and his finger prudently laid on the trigger of his gun, which was placed across his saddle-bow. His second day's ride was drawing to a close; he had left Arispe far behind him, which town he had passed through without stopping longer than he required to lay in fresh provisions and forage for his horse.

The sun was rapidly declining on the horizon; a rather powerful wind blew in gusts, raising clouds of dust, which blinded the horseman and formed a thick fog round him, in the midst of which he almost entirely disappeared. Although, as we have said, the day was drawing to a close, the heat was stifling, the sky had assumed a livid appearance; yellow clouds gradually collected in the horizon and were rapidly brought up by the wind. The birds whirled in the air, uttering shrill and discordant cries; sharp noises and shrill whistlings rose from among the rocks that on both sides flanked the narrow ravine the majordomo was now following, and large drops of rain fell on the calcined soil, which easily imbibed them. The horse pricked its ears, shook its head, and snorted in terror. All presaged one of those storms which it is only possible to witness in these regions—veritable cataclysms which rend and uproot the largest trees, force streams from their beds, and overthrow the soil, as if the earth were struggling wildly beneath the grasp of these horrible convulsions of Nature, which completely change within a few hours the aspect of the country over which they have swept with the fury of the African simoom.

"Hum!" José Paredes muttered to himself, as he took an anxious glance along the road; "if I am not greatly mistaken, within an hour we shall have one of the most tremendous *cordonazos* that has been seen for some time. That will be most agreeable for me, and my position will not fail to be most amusing. Confound the temporal! why could it not have waited for another eight-and-forty hours?"

The majordomo lost no time in vain lamentation. The situation in which he found himself was really critical: he knew that if the temporal surprised him on this ravine, he would have enormous difficulties to overcome in escaping its violence. He therefore resolved at all hazards to attempt the greatest efforts in getting out of the scrape. Minutes were precious; hesitation was impossible, and he must form a decision at once. José Paredes was a resolute man, long accustomed only to reckon on his courage, strength, and energy, to get him out of difficult situations; he therefore carefully wrapped himself in his zarapé, pulled his hat down over his forehead, and, bending over his horse's neck, dug his spurs, while crying, sharply, one word: "Santiago!" a cry employed in this country to excite horses. The noble animal, astonished that its master should deem it necessary to employ spurs to give it ardour, gave a snort of passion, and started at a headlong pace.

In the meanwhile the clouds had completely covered the blue sky; the atmosphere was gradually growing darker; the sunbeams had lost their heat; the horse still dashed on, rendered furious by the incessant prick of the spurs, which the majordomo dug into his panting flanks. At length Paredes uttered a cry of joy, for he had reached the end of the ravine, and before him extended a vast plain, bordered by tall mountains in the horizon. These mountains the majordomo wanted to reach, for there alone had he chance of safety. Although his position had greatly improved after leaving the ravine, it was still extremely difficult, if the storm were to burst before he had succeeded in crossing the plains, which afforded him no shelter to brave the tornado. Hence, the traveller, after exploring the neighbourhood with a rapid glance, and assuring himself that he had no hope of escaping the tempest, and the barren sandy plain which was only traversed by a few streams, repeated his cry of "Santiago," and set out on his mad ride once more.

As always happens, and as any one who has studied the admirable instinct of the horse can certify, the noble animal the major-domo rode seemed to have identified itself with its master. Through the effort of that magnetic current, whose power is no longer doubted, it appeared to understand that their common safety depended on its efforts; and it literally devoured the space, darting across the plain with the fantastic rapidity of the spectre steed of the German ballad.

All at once a vivid flash broke through the clouds, followed by a tremendous thunder-clap. The horse gave a start of terror, but quickly checked by its rider, started again through the torrents of rain which were beginning to fall. Night had suddenly set in; the sun, veiled by the clouds, had become invisible, and it was in complete obscurity that the majordomo was condemned to attempt the supreme efforts on which life or death depended. Still, Paredes was not discouraged, and his will seemed to grow fearless in the struggle; while sitting firmly in the saddle, like a granite statue, with contracted brows and eyes looking a-head, as if constantly trying to pierce the gloom, and exciting his horse with spur and voice, his features were as calm and impassive as if he were merely in one of the thousand ordinary accidents of his adventurous life in the desert. In the meanwhile the tempest had changed into a fearful hurricane, and raged with extreme fury. The unchained winds whistled violently, dashing the rain, and upraising masses of mud, which flew along the ground.

An ill-omened swashing made the unhappy traveller who was surprised by the tornado understand that the streams were beginning to overflow and inundate the plain. By the vivid flashes which uninterruptedly followed each other, the majordomo could see all around large grey pools of water, which constantly widened and enclosed him in an incessantly contracting circle; distant sounds borne by the breeze heightened his apprehensions. An hour more, he felt, and the plains would only form one vast lake, in the midst of which he would infallibly perish. Warned by that instinct which never deceives them, the wild beasts had left their lairs, and were flying madly, while uttering hoarse roars of terror. When a flash lit up the horizon, Paredes could see indistinct forms pass by his side which were no other than the dangerous denizens of the prairie. All was overthrown and confounded. The swash of the water was mingled with the artillery of the thunder and the howling of the wind. But the horse still galloped on straight ahead, sustained by the very terror which maddened it and spurred it on better than the sharpest knife could have done.

Suddenly the majordomo uttered a cry of terror and anger, drew himself up, and pulled bridle with such strength that the horse stopped short on his trembling legs. He fancied he had heard the distant sound of a bell. When an inundation comes, the haciendèros have all their bells rung, in order to warn straggling travellers and tell them of a place of refuge. The majordomo listened; in a few seconds a sound faint as a sigh reached the ear. The practised hunter was not mistaken; it was really the expiring sound of a bell that reached him, and the sound came from a direction diametrically opposite to the one he was following. In the darkness he had left his track; he was lost in the midst of an entirely submerged country without chance of help. In spite of his indomitable bravery the majordomo felt an internal horror; an icy perspiration stood on his forehead, and he shook all over. At this supreme moment the man had but one terrible thought that he would bear with him to the tomb the fortune entrusted to him by his master, and on which the future of his children perhaps depended. Paredes felt burning tears start from his eyes, and a choking sob from his bosom. He cared little for life: he would gladly have sacrificed it for his master; but the thought of dying thus, and completing his master's ruin, caused him indescribable grief. For some minutes this lion-hearted man, this bold woodranger, who had faced without blenching the most terrible dangers, felt weaker than a child. But this prostration only lasted a short time, and a reaction quickly took place; ashamed of the passing despondency to which he had yielded, the majordomo became the firmer when all seemed to abandon him, and resolved to sustain the insensate struggle till he drew his last breath.

Rendered stronger by this energetic resolution, the majordomo, whose arteries were beating as if about to burst, passed the back of his hand over his eyes, addressed to Heaven that mental prayer which the most intrepid men find in their hearts at the supreme moment when life or death only hangs by a thread; and, instead of going on, he waited for a flash, by which he could examine his position, and decide the new course he had to take. He had not to wait long; almost immediately a flash shot athwart the sky. Paredes uttered a cry of joy and surprise: he had seen, a few paces from him on his right, a rather tall hill, on the top of which he fancied he noticed a horseman, motionless, and upright as an equestrian statue.

With that coolness which powerful men

alone possess in critical circumstances, the majordomo, although he felt that the water was rapidly encircling him, and was almost up to his horse's girths, would not leave anything to chance. Fearing he had been deceived by one of those optical illusions, so frequent when the senses are over-excited, he resolved to wait for a second flash, and kept his eyes fixed on the spot where the hill must be, which he fancied he must have seen as in a dream. All at once, at the moment when the desired flash lit up the darkness, a voice, that overpowered the roar of the tempest, reached his ear:

"Courage! keep straight on," he heard.

The majordomo uttered a cry of delight, which resembled a yell; and, lifting his horse with his bridle and knees, he dashed toward the hill, pursued by the seething waters which were powerless to arrest him; and, after an ascent that lasted scarce ten minutes, he fell fainting in the arms of the man whose summons had saved him. From this moment he had nothing to fear: an inundation could not reach the top of the hill where he had found such a providential refuge.

CHAPTER XII.

A CONVERSATION BY NIGHT.

The majordomo's fainting fit, caused rather by the moral struggle he had sustained than by the physical fatigue he had endured, was not of any duration: when he re-opened his eyes, he was alone on the top of the hill. He threw off the furs and blankets laid over him, to protect him, doubtless, from the icy cold of the night, and looked curiously round him. The tempest was still raging, but it had lost a great deal of its violence. The rain had ceased: the deep blue sky was gradually becoming studded with twinkling stars, which shed an uncertain light, and gave the landscape an aspect of strange and desolate wildness. The wind blew furiously, and formed waves on the seething top of the waters, which had now almost risen to the spot where the majordomo lay. A few yards from its master, his horse was quietly grazing; it was eating the young tree shoots, and the tall close grass that covered the ground like a thick carpet of verdure. Another horse was browsing close by.

"Good!" Paredes muttered to himself, "my saviour has not gone away; I hope he is not far off, and that I shall see him soon. Where can he be? At his own business, of course, though I cannot guess the nature of his occupation at such a moment. Well, the best plan will be to wait for him."

The Mexican had scarce ended this soliloquy, ere a shadow stood out in the gloom, and the man of whom he was speaking appeared.

"Ah, ah!" he said, gaily, "you are all right again, I see: all the better; I would sooner have you in that position than the one you were in just now."

"Thanks," the majordomo cordially answered. "I fancy I must have looked very pitiable, stretched out like a half-throttled *novillo*. Is it not disgraceful for a strong man to faint like a child or a feeble woman?"

"Not the least in the world, *companero*," the other said, frankly. "Accident decreed that I should be for a long time the involuntary witness of the contest you waged, though it was impossible to help you, and *Viva Dios!* I declare that you are a tough combatant; you sustained the shock bravely, and many others in your place—I the first, perhaps—would not have got out of the scrape so well."

This answer completely broke the ice, and made the two men comparatively friends at once.

"I confess," Paredes remarked, as he offered his hand to his new friend, "that for a moment I believed myself lost, and had it not been for you I should have been so."

"Nonsense," the other replied, as he pressed the hand offered him. "You owe me nothing, for, by Jove! you saved yourself all alone. But let us not dwell on this point any longer. Although we are in relative safety, as the water cannot reach us here, our position is not the most agreeable; and I fancy it would be the best for us to try and get out of it as quickly as possible."

"That is my opinion, too; but, unluckily, the means at our disposal are very limited."

"Perhaps so; at any rate, with your consent, we will hold an Indian council."

"That is the best thing we can do at this moment. However," he added, as he looked up to the sky, "day will not break for three hours."

"We have time before us, in that case."

During this short conversation the storm had entirely ceased, and the wind only blew in gusts.

"Before all," the majordomo said, "let us light a fire; now that the tempest has ceased, the wild beasts, whose instinct is infallible, will seek the shelter of this hill, swarm round us, and, if we do not take care, carry our position by assault."

"Excellently argued; I see that you are a hunter."

"I was one for some time," Paredes replied, with a sigh of regret, "but now it is all over; my adventures in the desert are ended."

"I pity you sincerely," the stranger said, with an accent of sincerity; "for no existence is comparable with it."

"The finest years of my life were those I spent in the desert."

While conversing thus, the two men had dug a hole with their machetes at the foot of an enormous larch tree, to act as a hearth. In this hole they piled up all the resinous wood they were able to procure, lit it with some gunpowder rolled up in leaves, and in a few minutes a long jet of flame sprang up and joyously ascended to the sky, while the wood crackled and emitted millions of sparks. Fire has an immense influence upon the human mind; among other benefits, it has the faculty of restoring joy and hope; and while warming a man with its reviving heat, it often makes him forget perils incurred and fatigues endured. The two men, who were as wet as if they had been in a river, dried themselves for a considerable time, enjoying the pleasant sensations which the heat made them experience, in proportion as it penetrated into the pores, causing the blood to circulate with greater vivacity, and restoring elasticity to their benumbed limbs. It was the majordomo who was the first to resume the conversation.

"*Viva Dios!*" he said, shaking himself joyously; "I am now quite a different man.

What a fine thing a fire is when you are cold. Suppose we make use of it, comrade?"

"Do so, pray," the stranger replied, with a laugh; "but in what way?"

"Oh, that is very easy; you shall see. Are you not hungry?"

"*Caraï*, it is fourteen hours since I have eaten; but unluckily I have no provisions."

"Well, I have, and we will share them."

"Very good. I see that you are a first-rate fellow."

"The majordomo rose, fetched the alforjas which were fastened to his saddle, and then seated himself again by the fire.

"There!" he said, displaying his provisions with some degree of complacency.

"*Caramba!*" the other remarked, with a laugh; "food was never more welcome."

The provisions which caused such delight to the two men would have made our European goodwives smile with pity. They consisted of some slices of *tasajo*, *cicuia*, a lump of goat's cheese, and a few maize tortillas; but the majordomo produced a leather bottle, full of excellent mezcal, which had the privilege of restoring to the two adventurers all their merry carelessness.

The *tasajo* was laid on the coals, where it was soon done to a turn, and the two friends heartily attacked the supper. The frugal meal ended, they washed it down with a few sips of mezcal, fraternally passing the bottle to each other; then they lit their cigarettes, the *obligato* supplement of every Mexican repast, and began to smoke, while attentively surveying the heavy sky, which was already striped with dark bands under the influence of the early morning hours.

"Now, let us hold a council, if you are agreeable," the stranger said, as he inhaled an enormous mouthful of smoke, which he sent forth through his mouth and nostrils.

"As you are my senior on this territory," the majordomo remarked, with a laugh, "and are better acquainted with its resources than I am, you have the right to speak first."

"Very good: we are surrounded by water, and though the temporal has ceased, the streams will not return to their bed for several hours: moreover, the whole day will pass before the water is entirely absorbed by the sand."

"That is true," the majordomo said, with a significant shake of the head; "and yet we must get away from here."

"That is the question. To do so, we can only employ two means."

"Yes, we must either wait till the ground is dry, and that unfortunately will take a long time, which I cannot afford, as I am in a hurry: or at sunrise we can mount our horses, and bravely swim off, and reach the mountains, which cannot be very far distant."

"You forget another way which is still at our service."

"I do not think so."

"We can get into a canoe, and tow our horses after us, which will tire them less than carrying us; and enable us to reach the mountains to which you refer with greater ease; and they are only two leagues at the most, from this point."

"Your opinion is certainly good, and I approve of it with all my heart; unluckily we want one very important thing to carry it out."

"What is that?"

"Why, hang it all—the canoe."

"You are mistaken, *compadre*, we have one."

"Nonsense; how can that be possible?"

"While you were in a faint," the stranger continued, with a smile, "I explored our domain. You know that, in this country, when the rainy season arrives, the inhabitants are accustomed to hide canoes in bushes, and even in trees, in order to give travellers who are surprised by the inundation the means of saving themselves."

"That is true; have you found a canoe?"

"Yes; and hidden behind the very tree against which we are leaning."

"Heaven be praised! in that case we run no risk; but is the canoe in good condition?"

"I have assured myself of that fact, and even found two pairs of new paddles."

"Heaven is very certainly on our side. In that case we will start at sunrise, if that suits you."

"Excellently; though I am not in such a hurry as you appear to be, and for certain reasons I must remain in these parts for some days longer."

"Shall we employ the few hours left us in having a sleep?"

"You can sleep if you like, but as I am not at all fatigued, I shall watch over our common safety."

"I accept your proposal as frankly as you

make it. Yet, with your permission, I will not close my eyes till I have become better acquainted with you."

"How so? Are we not friends already?"

"Certainly, I am your friend, at least; but we do not know one another."

"That is to say——"

"We do not know one another—I mean, who we are."

"Oh, when travelling, what value can such formalities possess?"

"A greater value than you suppose; in a few hours we shall part, it is true, perhaps never to meet again; but perhaps, at some distant period, we may require each other's assistance; now, how could I summon you, if I did not know your name?"

"You're right, comrade; as for me, I am only a poor devil of a hunter, woodranger, or trapper—whichever you please, and my companions call me Stronghand, because, as they say, when I hold out my hand to a friend he can trust to it in perfect confidence."

"*Viva Dios*, caballero! you are well named, as I can declare; your reputation has already reached me, and I am delighted at the chance that has brought us together, as I had already desired to form your personal acquaintance."

"I thank you," the hunter replied, with a bow.

"As for me," the Mexican continued, "my name is José Paredes, and I am majordomo to the Marquis de Moguer."

"What!" Stronghand said, with a surprise he did not try to conceal; "you are the majordomo at the Hacienda del Toro?"

"Yes; what do you find surprising in that?"

"The man whom his master sent two days ago to Hermosillo, to receive cash for heavy bills drawn on an English banker?"

"How do you know that?" Paredes exclaimed, in his turn overwhelmed with surprise.

"What matter, so long as I know it?" the hunter replied. "Believe me," he added, with an accent that caused the majordomo deep reflection, "our meeting is truly providential, and Heaven led us towards each other."

"That is strange," Paredes muttered; "how is it possible that a secret which my master confided to me alone should be in your possession?"

The hunter smiled. "A secret known to three persons," he said, "does not long remain a secret."

"But that third person, to whom you refer, has no right to divulge it."

"How do you know that? I will say to you, in my turn, Master Paredes. Sufficient for you, for the present, to learn that I am aware of the cause of your journey. I think you said you had heard speak of me before we met?"

"That is true, Senor."

"What terms did the persons who spoke of me employ?"

"The best, I must allow. They represented you to me as a man of unspotted loyalty and dauntless courage."

"Good! Does that report satisfy you—have you confidence in me?"

"Yes; for I am convinced that you are an honest man."

"I hope that your opinion of me will not alter. I will soon prove to you that it is fortunate for you and the Marquis that we have met at the moment when you least expected it; for I was looking for you."

"Looking for me? I do not understand you."

"You do not require to understand me at the present moment; but set your mind at rest, everything will be explained ere long."

"I hope so."

"And I am certain of it. Are you devoted to your master?"

"My family have lived on the estate for two hundred years."

"That is not a reason; answer distinctly."

"I am devoted to him body and soul, and would willingly lay down my life for him."

"That is the way to answer; however, I knew it already, and only desired that your lips should confirm what I have been told."

"My master has no secrets from me."

"I know that also. Well, now, listen to me attentively, Senor Paredes, for what I have to reveal to you is of the utmost gravity."

"I am listening to you, Senor."

"Your master is at this moment in danger

of being utterly ruined. He is the plaything of villains who have sworn to destroy him. The sum you are going to fetch they intend to take from you, and everything is prepared to make you fall into an infamous trap, in which you will infallibly perish."

"Are you certain of what you assert?" the majordomo exclaimed, in horror.

"I know all, I repeat to you: the men from whom I obtained your secret, who little expected that I was listening to them, at the same time revealed to me the means they intended to employ in assassinating you."

"Why, that is infamous!"

"I am completely of your opinion, and that is why, instead of setting my traps in the desert, as I ought to be doing, I am now here. I wish to foil the plots of these villains, and confound them."

"But what interest induces you to act thus?" the majordomo asked, with a shadow of distrust.

"That question I cannot answer. You must for the present lay aside all curiosity; you must place entire confidence in me, and give me, in what I propose doing, as much help as I shall offer you. Does this suit you? I fancy that the bargain I offer is entirely to your advantage, and that you will run no risk beyond what I do myself."

There was a lengthened silence. The majordomo was reflecting on what he had just heard, while the hunter, with his eyes fixed on him, was patiently waiting till he thought proper to renew the conversation. At length Paredes raised his head, and held out his hand to the hunter, who pressed it.

"Listen, Stronghand," he said to him: "all that you have told me appears extraordinary, and I confess that at once; but there is such frankness in your voice, and your reputation is so well established among your brethren, the woodrangers, who all proclaim your loyalty, that I do not hesitate to confide in you without any reservation, for I am convinced that you can have no idea of betraying me, up to the moment when you think proper to reveal to me the names of the villains into whose hands I should have infallibly fallen, had it not been for you, and who have sworn the ruin of my beloved master. I will do what you ask of me, resign my will entirely; you may regard me as a thing belonging entirely to you. Come, go, act as you think proper, and I will obey you in everything, without asking any explanation of your conduct. Now, in your turn, say if it suits you."

"Yes, my worthy friend, that pleases me. You have guessed my thought: I require this liberty to give me the means of succeeding in what I wish to do. Believe the word of an honest man. If anything can add to the confidence you have placed in me, and of which I am proud, I swear to you, by all that is most sacred in the world, that no one is more interested than I am in the Marquis de Moguer, or more sincerely desires to see him happy."

"We shall still start at sunrise, eh?"

"Yes; but not to proceed to Hermosillo. Before going to that town, we must take certain indispensable precautions. We have to deal with the most crafty bandits on the border, and must beat them by cunning. They are on our track, and we must cheat the cheaters."

"Good, good; I will call to mind my old hunter's profession."

"Remember, above all, the prairie proverb, that 'The trees have eyes and the leaves ears.' Fortunately for us, the villains who are watching for you do not disturb me in any way; I reckon principally on that ignorance to foil their plots."

"But if we do not go to Hermosillo, where are we going?"

"To-morrow, when it is daylight," the hunter answered sententiously, "when the bright sunbeams permit me to convince myself that no one can hear us, I will tell you. For the present, sleep, rest yourself, so that you may be able to support the fatigue that awaits you."

And, as if to avoid fresh questioning, the hunter wrapped himself in his zarape, leant his back against the larch tree, stretched out his legs to the fire, and closed his eyes. The majordomo, in spite of his lively desire to continue the conversation, imitated him; and a few minutes later, overcome by the fatigue of every description he had endured for some days, he was fast asleep.

CHAPTER XIII.

THE REAL DE MINAS.

For some years past—that is to say, since the day when Captain Sutter, while digging a well at his plantation in San Francisco, accidentally found a lump of virgin gold—the discovery of the rich mines of the New World has so aroused interest and excited admiration, by giving a fresh impulse to avarice and covetousness, that we consider it necessary to say a few words here about the mines. Of course we shall allude to those situated in the country where our scene is laid—that is, in Sonora.

Sonora is the richest mining country in the world. We assured ourself by official data that six hundred bars of silver and sixty bars of gold, worth together a million of piastres, were brought to the Mint of Hermosillo in 1839. To this large amount a nearly equal sum must be added, which is not brought to be assayed, in order to avoid the payment of the duty, which is five per cent. on silver and four per cent. on gold. This country also possesses most valuable copper mines, but the population generally abandons the other metals to seek virgin gold.

No country in the world possesses auriferous strata so rich and so extensive (*criaderos* or *placeres d'oro*). The metal is found in alluvial soil in ravines after rain, and always on the surface or at a depth of a few feet. In the north of the province of Arispe, the placers of Quitoval and Sonoitac, which were found again in 1836, and to which we shall soon have to allude more specially, produced for three years two hundred ounces of gold per day,—that is to say, reducing it to our money, the large sum of two hundred and fifty thousand pounds.

The gold-seekers restrict themselves to turning up the soil with a pointed stick, and only collect the nuggets that are visible; but if the streams were diverted from their course, and large washings undertaken, the profits would be far more considerable. It is not rare to find nuggets weighing several pounds; we saw at Arispe, in the hands of a miner, one that was worth nine thousand piastres, or about eighteen hundred pounds; and the Royal Cabinet at Madrid contains several magnificent specimens. We will soon describe how and why the working of these strata was interrupted.

Most of the buildings of the *pueblos*, or Missions of Sonora, serve as the gathering-place of the nomadic workmen and traders who collect round any important mine so soon as its working is begun. The place where the workmen assemble takes the name of *Real de Minas* or *Mineral;* and if the mine promises to be productive for any length of time, the population definitively settles round it. Many important towns of Mexico had no other origin. The facility with which the miners earn large sums explains the enormous consumption of European goods which takes place in the provinces. Simple rancheros may frequently be seen spending in a few days seven or eight pounds of gold, which only cost them a week's toil. Unhappily, the ruinous passion for gambling—that shameful leprosy of Mexico, whose inhabitants it degrades—prevents the great mine-owners from keeping a large capital on their hands, and thus checks works on a great scale.

Before resuming our narrative, we must also give the reader certain information about the Indian nations that inhabit the territory of Sonora. There are in this province five distinct tribes: the Yaquis, the Opatas, the Mayos, the Gilenos, and the Apaches. The Yaquis and Mayos occupy the country to the south of Guaymas, as far as the Rio del Huerto; they let themselves out to the creoles as farm-labourers, masons, servants, miners, and divers. Their number is about forty thousand. The Opatas reside along the bank of the San Miguel de Horcasitos, the Arispe, the Los Ures, and the Oposina; they are very good workmen and excellent soldiers. They have always served the government faithfully, both Spanish and Mexican, and their number is estimated at thirty thousand.

The Gilenos spread along the banks of the Gila and Colorado rivers. The Axuas and Apaches, who belong to the Sierra Madre, are confounded under the name of Papazos. These Indians are nomadic, and only live by hunting and plunder; they were formerly encamped to the north of

Chihuahua and Sonora; but being driven back by the progress of the Americans and Texans, they threw themselves upon the Mexican territory, where they cause immense damage, for they are well supplied with fire-arms, which they obtained in exchange for peltry and cattle at the American establishments of the Arkansas, the Missouri, and the Rio Bravo del Norte. In order to complete this brief enumeration of the Indian nations of Sonora, we will mention a mission established at the gates of Hermosillo, and in which five hundred Seris Indians lived; a thousand members of the same tribe, formerly one of the most powerful in this country, but now almost extinct, dwelt on the coast to the north of Guaymaz, and in Tiburon or Sharkesland.

We will now temporarily leave Stronghand and José Paredes at the top of the hill, where they found a shelter from the inundation, and lead the reader to the Real de Minas of Quitoval, where certain important events are about to take place.

It was the evening: the streets and plazas of the pueblo were crowded with individuals of every description: Yaquis Indians, hunters, miners, gambusinos, monks, and adventurers, who composed the motley population of the Mineral, mounted and foot, incessantly jostled each other, and bowed, spoke, laughed, or quarrelled. Some were returning from the placer, where they had been at work all day; others were leaving their houses to enjoy the evening breeze; others, and they were the larger number, were entering the drinking shops, through whose doors could be heard the songs of the topers, and the shrill, inharmonious tinkling jarabes and vihuelas.

One of these *tendajos*, of a more comfortable and less dirty appearance than the rest, seemed to have the privilege of attracting a greater number of customers than all the rival establishments. After passing through a low door and descending two steps of unequal height, the visitor found himself in a species of hideous den, resembling at once a cellar and a shed, whose earthen flooring, rendered uneven by the mud constantly brought in by customers, caused persons to stumble at each step who visited the place for the first time. A hot heavy vapour, impregnated with alcoholic fumes and mephitic exhalations, escaped through the door of this den, as from the mouth of Hades, and painfully affected mouth and eyes, before the latter became accustomed to the close, obscure aspect of the place, and were enabled to pierce the thick curtain of vapour, which was constantly drawn from one side to the other by the movements of the customers. They perceived, by the dubious light of a few *candils* scattered here and there, a large and lofty room, whose once whitewashed walls had become black at the lower part by the constant friction of heads, backs, and shoulders, to which they served as a support.

Facing the door was a daïs, raised about a foot above the ground; this daïs occupied the entire width of the room, and was divided into two parts; that on the right contained a table forming a bar, behind which stood a tall, active fellow, with false look and ill-tempered face, the master of the tendajo. Above the head of this respectable personage, who answered to the harmonious name of Cospeto, a niche had been made in the wall, in which was a statue of the Virgin, holding the Holy Infant in her arms; in front of the statue a dozen small wax tapers, fixed on a row of iron points, were burning. The left hand portion of the daïs was occupied by the musicians, or performers on jarabes and vihuelas.

On each side of the room, the centre of which remained free for the dancers, ran rickety, badly-made, and dirty tables, occupied at this moment by a crowd of customers, some seated on benches, others standing, laughing, talking, shouting, quarrelling; drinking mezcal, refino, pulque, or infusion of tamarinds, or else staking at monte the gold earned during the day at the mine, and which their dirty hands fetched from the pockets of the shapeless rags that served them as garments. A few women, creatures without a name, whose features were sodden with debauchery, and eyes deep sunk with drinking, were mingled with the crowd; and all, both men and women, were smoking either cigars or husk cigarettes.

Nothing can describe the hideous aspect of this infamous Pandemonium, the refuge of all the vices of the province, overlooked by the gentle, smiling face of the statue of the Virgin, whose features, in the light of the tapers, assumed an expression of wondrous pity and sorrow.

At the moment when we invite the

reader to enter this drinking shop with us the fun was at its height, the room was full of drinkers and dancers, and the whole mob laughed, yelled, and made a row which would have rendered the saint herself deaf. On the left, near the door, a man, wrapped up in a thick cloak, one end of which was raised to his face, and completely concealed his features, was sitting motionless at a separate table, looking absently and carelessly at the dancers who whirled round him. When a new comer entered the tendajo, this man looked toward the door, and then turned his head away with an air of ill-humour when he perceived that the new comer was not the person that he had been so long expecting, for he had been sitting alone at this table for upwards of two hours. Still no one paid, or seemed to pay, any attention to him—all were too much absorbed in their own occupations to think about a man who obstinately remained gloomy and silent amid this revelry. The stranger, so often deceived in his expectations, at length gave up looking toward the door; he let his head fall on his chest and went to sleep, or pretended to do so, either for the sake of not attracting attention, or else to indulge with greater freedom in his reflections.

All at once a formidable disturbance broke out at one end of the room; a table was upset by a vigorous blow; oaths crossed each other in the air, and knives were drawn from boots; musicians and dancers stopped short, and a circle was formed round two men who, with frowning brows, eyes sparkling with intoxication and passion, a zarape rolled as a buckler round the left arm, and a navaja in their right hand, were preparing, according to all appearance, to attack each other vigorously. The tendajero, or master of the house, then proved himself equal to the position he occupied—he leaped like a jaguar over the counter behind which he had hitherto stood coldly and indifferently, merely engaged in watching his waiters and serving customers; he closed the front door, against which he leant his powerful shoulders, in order to prevent any customer bolting without payment of his score, and prepared with evident interest to witness the fight.

The two men, with outstretched legs, left arm advanced, bodies bent forward, and knife held by the middle of the blade, were standing looking in each other's eyes, ready for attack, defence, or parry. All at once the mysterious sleeper appeared to wake with a start, as if surprised by the voice of one of the adversaries, took a hasty glance at the combatants, and then darted between them.

"What is the matter?" he asked, in a firm voice, the sound of which affected the duellists, who were astounded at an interference they had been far from expecting.

"This man," one of them answered, "has lost three ounces to me at monté, through the unexpected turn up of the ace of spades."

"Well?" the stranger interjected.

"He refuses to pay me," the gambler continued; "because he declares that the cards were packed, and that consequently I cheated him, which is not true, for—*viva Dios!* I am known to be a caballero."

At this affirmation, which was slightly erroneous, a smile of singular meaning, but which no one saw, curled the stranger's lip; he continued, in a most serious voice—

"It is true that you are a caballero, and I would affirm it were it necessary; but the most honest man is subject to deceive himself, and I am convinced that this has happened to you. Hence, instead of fighting with this caballero, whose honour and loyalty cannot either be doubted, prove to him that you recognise your error by paying him the three ounces, which you claimed of him through an oversight; this gentleman will apologize for having used certain ugly expressions, and all will then be settled to the general satisfaction."

"Certainly, I am convinced that this caballero is a man of honour: I am ready to proclaim it anywhere, and I regret with all my soul the misunderstanding which momentarily divided us," said the individual who had not yet spoken, though he remained on the defensive, a position that slightly contradicted the apparent good-humour of his remark.

The stranger then turned to the man whose friend he had so unexpectedly made himself, and gave him a sign which the other appeared to understand.

"Well, caballero," he said, with an irony whose expression was hardly noticeable, "what do you think of this apology? For my part, I consider it complete and most honourable."

The man thus addressed hesitated for a moment; a combat was evidently going on in his mind; his furious glances seemed to challenge the company; and had he perceived on the face of one of the spectators an expression of contempt, however fugitive it might have been, he would doubtless have immediately picked another quarrel. But all the persons who surrounded him were cold and indifferent; curiosity alone was legible on their features. He unrolled his cloak, returned the knife to his boot, and held out his hand to his adversary at the same time that he gave him three ounces.

"Pardon me an involuntary error at which I am truly confused," he said, with a courteous bow, but with a sigh he could not restrain.

The other took the ounces without pressing, thrust them away in his capacious pockets with far from ordinary dexterity, returned the salute, and mingled with the crowd, who, through a lengthened acquaintance with the two men, did not at all comprehend this peaceful result.

"Now, Master Kidd," the stranger continued, as he laid his hand on the shoulder of the adventurer, who stood motionless in the middle of the room, "I suppose that all your business here is settled; so, with your permission, we will withdraw."

"As you please," Kidd answered, carelessly, for this man was no other than the bandit we came across in the opening of our story.

The groups had broken up, the crowd had dispersed, musicians and dancers had returned to their places, and the two men could consequently leave without attracting attention. The stranger, when he reached the purer atmosphere of the street, took several deep inspirations, as if trying to expel from his lungs the vitiated air he had been constrained to swallow for so long. Then he turned to his companion, who was walking silently by his side.

"*Cuerpo de Cristo!* Master Kidd," he said, in a tone of ill-humour, "you are, it must be confessed, a singular fellow; you compel me, the commandant of this pueblo, to come and hunt you up at this filthy den, where, on your entreaty, I consented to meet you, and instead of watching for my arrival, you leave me among the most perfect collection of bandits I ever saw in my life."

"Excess of zeal, captain; so you must not be angry with me for that," the bandit answered, with a cunning look. "In order to be punctual at the rendezvous I gave you, I had been for nearly four hours at worthy Senor Cospeto's. Not knowing how to spend my time, I played at cards. You know what monté is; once I have the cards in my hand, and the gold on the table, I forget everything."

"Good, good," the stranger answered. "I am willing to believe you. Still, I pledge you my word, that if you dupe me in the affair you have proposed, and the information you offer to sell me is false, you will repent it. You know me, I think, Master Kidd?"

"Yes, Captain Don Marcos de Niza, and I suppose that you know me too; but of what use is this discussion? Let us settle our business first, and then you can act as you think proper."

The Captain gave him a suspicious glance.

"It is well," he said, as he rapped at a door; "come in, this is my house; I prefer treating with you here to the tendajo."

"As you please," the bandit said, and followed the Captain into his house, the doors of which were closed behind them.

CHAPTER XIV.

THE BARGAIN.

Captain Don Marcos de Niza, whom we left commanding the post of San Miguel, and defending it against the Indians, had been a few days previously summoned to the political and military government of the Mineral of Quitoval, by an order that arrived from Mexico, and emanated from the President of the Republic himself. The fact was, that during the last few days certain events had occurred which demanded energetic action on the part of the President. All at once, at a moment when no discontent was supposed to exist among the Indians, the latter, after long councils they had held together, revolted, and had, without any declaration of war, invaded the Mexican territory at several points simultaneously. This revolt suddenly assumed serious proportions; and had become the more formidable within a short time, because the revolters were the Gilenos, that is to say, the Comanches, Apaches, and Axuas, whose dangerous country is known by the name of the Papazos.

The General commanding Sonora and Cinaloa, the two states most exposed to the depredations of the Indians, saw that he must oppose to the Indians a man who, through a lengthened residence on the borders, had acquired great experience as to their way of fighting and the tricks they employ. Only one officer fulfilled these conditions, and that officer was Captain de Niza; he, therefore, received orders to quit the post of San Miguel after dismantling it, and proceed immediately to the Mineral of Quitoval. The Captain obeyed with that promptitude which old soldiers alone can display in the execution of the orders they receive. His first care, on reaching the Mineral, was to protect the pueblo, as far as was possible, from a surprise, by digging a large trench, throwing up entrenchments, and barricading the principal streets.

Unfortunately the general commanding the provinces had but a very limited military force at his disposal; scarce amounting to six hundred infantry and two hundred cavalry, without field artillery. Hence, in spite of his lively desire to give the Captain a respectable force, as he was obliged to scatter his troops along the whole seaboard of the two states, he found it impossible to send to Quitoval more than one hundred infantry and fifty cavalry. In spite of the numerical weakness of his troops the Captain did not despair. He was one of those men to whom the performance of duty was everything; and who carry out without a murmur the most extraordinary order.

Still, as he expected to be attacked at any moment by an army of ten or fifteen thousand veteran Indians, amply supplied with firearms, and who, through being accustomed to fight with Spaniards, could not be easily terrified, he had to augment the number of his soldiers, so as to have men enough to line the entrenchments he had thrown up round the town. He had two means by which to obtain this result, and he employed them. The first consisted in making the great mine owners understand that they must participate in the defences of the pueblo, either personally or by arming and placing under his orders a certain number of the peons they employed; for if the Indians succeeded in seizing the Mineral, the source of their wealth would be at once dried up.

The great owners understood the Captain's reasons the more easily because their interests were at stake; they therefore enthusiastically followed his advice, and raised at their common charge a corps of one hundred and fifty Opatas—brave soldiers, thoroughly devoted to the Whites. They placed this corps under the Captain's orders, pledging themselves to pay and support it so long as the danger lasted. Don Marcos thus doubled his army at one stroke. This success, which he had been far from expecting, owing to his profound knowledge of the apathy and selfishness of his countrymen, induced him to try the second plan.

This was very simple. It consisted in enlisting, for a certain bounty, as many as he could of the adventurers who always swarm on the borders, and whose neutrality is at times more formidable than declared enmity. The sum offered by the Captain was two ounces per man, one payable on enlistment, the other at the termination of the campaign. This offer, seductive though it was, did not produce all the effect the Captain expected from it. The adventurers responded but feebly to the appeal made to them. These men in whose hearts patriotic love does not exist, and who only care for pillage, saw in the insurrection of the Indians a source of disorder, and, consequently, of rapine. They cared very little about defending a state of things which their predacious instincts led them, on the contrary, to attack.

Thirty or forty adventurers, however, responded to the call, and these immoral men, who were impatient at the yoke of discipline, were rather an embarrassment than an assistance to the Captain; still as, take them altogether, they were sturdy fellows, and thoroughly acquainted with Indian warfare, he attached them to his cavalry, which was thus raised to a strength of one hundred men. Don Marcos thus found himself at the head of two hundred and fifty infantry and one hundred horse—a force which appeared to him, if well directed, more than sufficient to withstand, behind good entrenchments, the effort of the whole Indian army.

We are aware that this number of men defending a town will produce a smile of pity among European readers, who are accustomed to see on battle-fields masses of three hundred thousand men come into collision. But all is relative in this world. In America, where the population is comparatively small, great things have often been decided at the bayonet's point by armies whose relative strength did not exceed that of one of our line regiments. In the last battle fought between the Texans and Mexicans—a battle which decided the independence of Texas, the two armies together did not amount to two thousand men, and yet the collision was terrible, and victory obstinately disputed. In the actions between white men and Indians, the latter, in spite of their indomitable valour, were almost always defeated in a pitched battle, in spite of their crushing superiority of numbers. Not through the courage of their enemies, but by their discipline and military skill. The latter is certainly very limited, but sufficient for adversaries such as they have to combat.

One night, when the Captain returned home after his usual visit to the pueblo to assure himself that all was in order, a ragged lepero, more than half intoxicated with mezcal and pulque, handed him with an infinitude of bows, a dirty slip of paper folded up in the shape of a letter. Don Marcos de Niza was not accustomed to neglect anything. He attached as much importance to apparently frivolous events as to those which seemed to possess a certain gravity. He stopped, took the letter, gave a real to the lepero, who went away quite satisfied, and entered his house, which was situated on the Plaza Mayor, in the centre of the pueblo.

After throwing his cap and sword on a table, the Captain opened the letter. He read it at first rather carelessly; but ere long he began frowning, and read the letter a second time, attentively weighing each word. Then at the end of a moment he folded up the letter, and said in a low voice—

"I will go."

This letter came from Kidd. The Captain had been long acquainted with the bandit, and knew certain peculiar facts about him which would have been most disagreeable to the bandit, had the latter suspected that the Captain was so thoroughly initiated in the secrets of his vagabond life. Hence Don Marcos fancied he had no right to neglect the overtures the other was pleased to make; while keeping on his guard and determined to punish him severely if he deceived him. The Captain, therefore, proceeded without hesitation to the place where the adventurer appointed to meet him. He had waited for him for several hours with exemplary patience, and would probably have waited longer still, had not chance suddenly brought them face to face in the way we have described.

When the two men had entered the house, and the door closed after them, Don Marcos de Niza, still closely followed by the bandit, who, in spite of his impudence, looked around him timidly, like a wolf caught in a sheep-fold, led him into a room the door of which he carefully closed. The Captain pointed to a chair, sat down at a table, laid a brace of pistols ostentatiously within his reach, and said—

"Now I am ready to hear you."

"*Caraï?*" the bandit said, impudently; "that is possible; but the point is whether I am disposed to speak."

"And why not, pray, my excellent friend?"

"Hang it, Captain," he said, as he pointed to the pistols; "there are two playthings not at all adapted to set my tongue wagging."

Don Marcos looked at him in a way that

made the adventurer involuntarily let his eyes fall, and then leant his elbows on the table.

"Master Kidd," he then said, in a stern voice, though a certain tone of sarcasm was perceptible in it, "I like a distinct understanding; let us therefore, before anything establish our relative positions. You have led a very agitated life, Master Kidd; your vagabond humour, your mad desire to appropriate certain things to which you have a very dubious claim have led you into a few mistakes, whose results might prove remarkably disagreeable to you."

The bandit shook his head in denial.

"I will not dwell," the Captain continued, mockingly, "on a subject which must make your modesty greatly suffer, and will come at once to the motives of your presence here, and the positions we must hold toward each other. I am commandant of this pueblo, and in that capacity compelled to watch over its external safety as well as its internal tranquillity, I think you will agree with me."

"Yes, Captain," the bandit answered, somewhat reassured at finding the conversation turned away from such delicate topics.

"Very good; you wrote me this letter,

appointing a meeting and offering to sell—that is your own word—certain most important information, as you say, for the continuance of the safety and tranquillity which I am bound to maintain. Another man might have treated you in the Indian fashion. After having you arrested, he would have ordered a cord to be fastened round your temples; or your suspension by your thumbs—as you have done yourself, if report be true, on various occasions with less valid reasons; and have so thoroughly loosened your tongue that you would not have kept a single secret back. I have preferred dealing with you as an honest man."

The bandit breathed again.

"Still, as you are one of those persons with whom it is advisable to take precautions, and in whom a confidence cannot be placed, as they would not scruple to abuse it on the first opportunity, I retain not only the right, but also the means of blowing out your brains if you have the slightest intention of deceiving me."

"Oh, Captain, what an idea! Blow out my brains!" the bandit stammered.

"Do you fancy, my dear Senor," the Captain continued, still sarcastically, "that your friends will pity you greatly, if such a misfortune happened to you?"

"Hum! to tell you the truth, I do not exactly know," the adventurer answered, with an attempt to jest; "people are so unkind. But, since you accept the bargain offered to you—for you do accept it, I think, Captain?"

"I do."

"What, then, will you give me in exchange for what I shall tell you?"

"You sell; I buy; it is your place to make your conditions, and, if they are not exorbitant—if, in a word, they seem to me fair, I will accept them; so, speak, what do you ask?"

"*Caraï!* Captain; it is a delicate question, for I am an honest man."

"That is allowed," Don Marcos interrupted him with a laugh. "Name your price."

"Fifty ounces; would that be too much?" the bandit ventured.

"Certainly not, if the thing be worth it."

"Then," Kidd exclaimed, joyfully, "that is understood, fifty ounces.

"I repeat, if it be worth it."

"Oh, you shall judge for yourself," he remarked, rubbing his hands.

"I ask nothing better but to buy, and to prove to you that I have no intention of cheating you," he added, as he opened a drawer and took out a rather heavy purse, "here is the amount."

And the Captain made two piles each of twenty-five ounces, exactly between the pistols. At the sight of the gold the bandit's eyes sparkled like those of a wild beast.

"*Ravo de Dios!* Captain," he exclaimed; "there is a pleasure in treating with you. I will remember it another time."

"I ask nothing better, Master Kidd. Now speak, I am listening."

"Oh, I have not much to say; but you will judge whether it is important."

"Go on; I am all ears."

"In two words, this is the matter; the Papazos have not elected a chief, but an emperor!"

"An emperor?"

"Yes."

"What do they assert, then?"

"They mean to be free, and wish to constitute their independence upon a solid basis."

"Do you know this emperor?"

"I have seen him, at least."

"Who is he?"

"A man who is the more formidable because he appears to belong to the white rather than the red race; and is thoroughly conversant with all the means hitherto employed by the Indians."

"Is he young?"

"He is sixty; but as active as if he were only twenty."

"Very good; proceed."

"Is that important?"

"Very important. But not worth fifty ounces, for all that."

"The Yaquis, Mayos, and Seris have allowed themselves to be seduced, and have entered the Confederation. They have taken up again their old plans of 1827—you remember, at the time of their great revolution?"

"Yes; go on."

"The first expedition the Chief of the Confederation means to undertake is the capture of the Real de Minas."

"I am aware of it."

"Yes; but do you know, Captain, that the Indians have spies even among the garrison; that all is ready for the attack, and that the Papazos intend to surprise you within the next two days?"

"Who gave you this information?"

The bandit smiled craftily.

"What use my telling you, Captain," he answered, "if the information is correct?"

"Do you know the men who have entered into negotiations with the enemy?"

"I do."

"In that case tell me their names."

"It would be imprudent, Captain."

"Why so?"

"Judge for yourself. Suppose I were to tell you their names, what would happen?"

"*Viva Dios!*" the Captain sharply interrupted him. "I should shoot them like the miserable dogs they are, and to serve as a warning to others."

"Well, that is the mistake, Captain."

"How a mistake?"

"Why, yes; suppose you shoot ten men?"

"Twenty, if necessary!"

"Say twenty, it is of no consequence to me; but those who remain, whom neither you nor I know, will sell you to the Indians, so that the only result will be precipitating the evil instead of preventing it."

"Ah, ah!" the Commandant said, with an expressive glance at the bandit. "And what would you do in my place?"

"Oh, a very simple thing."

"Well, what is it?"

"I would leave the scamps at liberty to prepare their treachery, while carefully watching them; and when the moment for attack arrived, I would have them quietly arrested; so that the Indians would be surprised instead of surprising us, and we should cheat the cunning cheats."

The Captain appeared to reflect for a moment, and then said—

"The plan you recommend seems to me good, and for the present I see no inconvenience in carrying it out. Give me the names of the traitors."

Kidd mentioned a dozen names, which the Captain wrote down after him.

"Now," Don Marcos continued, "there are your fifty ounces, and I shall give as many each time you bring me information as valuable as that of to-day. I pay you dearly, so it is your interest to serve me faithfully; but remember, that if you deceive me, nothing can save you from the punishment I will inflict on you, and that punishment, I warn you, will be terrible."

The adventurer bounded on the money like a wild beast on a prey it has long coveted, concealed it with marvellous dexterity in his wide pockets, and said to the Captain with a bow—

"Senor Don Marcos, I have always thought that in this world gold was the sovereign master, and that it alone had the right to command."

After accompanying these singular words with a smiling and almost mocking expression, Kidd bowed for the last time and disappeared, leaving the Captain to his reflections.

CHAPTER XV.

THE PAPAZOS.

WE will now return to Stronghand and José Paredes, whom we have left too long at the top of the hill. The night passed without any incident; the majordomo sleeping like a man overcome by fatigue; as for the hunter, he did not close his eyes once. The sun had risen for a long time; it was nearly nine o'clock, but the hunter, forgetting apparently what he had said to his comrade, did not dream of departure. José Paredes slept on. It was a magnificent day; the sky, swept by the night hurricane, was cloudless; the sun darted down its glowing beams; and yet the atmosphere, tempered by the storm, retained an agreeable freshness. The water was disappearing with a rapidity almost equalling that it had displayed in rising, being drunk by the thirsty sand or by the hot sunbeams; the plain had lost its lacustrine appearance; and all led to the supposition that by midday the ground would be firm enough to be ventured on in safety.

As the canoe was unnecessary, the hunter did not try to get it down from the tree; with his back leant against the larch tree, his hands folded, and his head bowed on his chest, he was thinking, and at times taking an anxious glance at his sleeping comrade. At length the majordomo turned, stretched out his arms and legs, opened his eyes, and gave a formidable yawn.

"*Caramba!*" he said, as he measured the height of the sun; "I fancy I have forgotten myself; it must be very late."

"Ten o'clock," the hunter answered with a smile.

"Ten o'clock!" José exclaimed, as he leaped up; "and you have let me idle thus instead of waking me."

"You slept so soundly, my friend, that I had not the courage to do so."

"Hum!" Paredes replied, half-laughing, half-vexed; "I know not whether I ought to complain or thank you for this weakness, for we have lost precious time."

"Not at all; see, the water has disappeared; the ground is growing firm again, and when the great heat of the day is spent we will mount our horses and catch up in a few hours the time you are regretting."

"That is true, and you are right, comrade," said the majordomo, as he looked around with the practised glance of a man accustomed to a desert life. "Well, as it is so," he added, with a laugh, "suppose we breakfast, for that will enable us to kill some time."

"Very good," the hunter replied, good humouredly.

They breakfasted as they had supped on the previous night. When the hour for starting at length arrived, they saddled their horses and led them down the hill; for the ascent which they had escaladed so actively by night, under the impulse of the pressing danger that threatened them, now proved extremely steep, abrupt, and difficult. When they mounted, Stronghand said—

"My friend, I am going to take you to an *atepetl* of the Red-skins. Do you consider that disagreeable?"

"Not personally, but I will ask what advantage my master can derive from it?"

"That question I am unable to answer at the moment. You must know, though, that we are taking this step on your master's behalf, and that his affairs, instead of suffering by it, will be greatly benefited."

"Let us go, then. One word, however, first. Are the Red-skins, to whom we are proceeding, a long distance off?"

"It would be almost a journey for any persons but us."

"Hum!" said Paredes.

"But you and I," the hunter continued, "who are true guides, and who have also the advantage of being well mounted, will reach the village at three or four o'clock to-morrow afternoon at the latest."

"In that case it is not very distant?"

"I told you so."

"And in what direction is the village?"

"You must have often heard it spoken of, if chance has never led your footsteps thither."

"Why so?"

"Because it is only a dozen leagues at the most from the Hacienda del Toro."

"Wait a minute," the majordomo said, frowning like a man who is collecting his thoughts; "you are right, I have never been to that village, it is true, but I have often heard it spoken of. Is not one of the chiefs a white man?"

The hunter blushed slightly.

"So people say," he answered.

"Is it not strange," the majordomo continued, "that a white man should consent to abandon entirely the society of his fellows to live with savages?"

"Why so?"

"Hang it! because the Indians are devoid of reason, as everybody knows."

The hunter gave his companion a glance of indefinable meaning, slightly shrugged his shoulders, but made no reply; probably from the reason that he had too much to say, and considered the majordomo's rather heavy mind incapable of appreciating it. The day passed without any occurrences to interrupt the monotony of their ride, which they continued with great speed till night, only stopping from time to time to shoot a few birds for supper. Galloping, talking, and smoking, they at length reached the spot where they intended to bivouac. The road they had followed in no way resembled the one the majordomo had taken on leaving the hacienda, although they were returning in the direction of Arispe. This resulted from the fact that Paredes had kept in the regular road, while this time the two men rode Indian fashion, that is to say, straight a-head without troubling themselves about roads. They galloped on as the bird flies, crossing mountains and swimming rivers whenever they came to them, without losing time in seeking a ford.

This mode of travelling, generally adopted by the woodrangers of the savannah, where the only roads are tracks made by the wild beasts, would not be possible in civilized countries, where there are so many towns and villages; but in Mexico, especially on the Indian border, towns are excessively rare: by riding in this way distances are marvellously shortened and a considerable tract is covered between two sunrises. This is what happened to the two adventurers; for in one day they went a greater distance than Paredes had done in eight-and-forty hours, though he was well mounted. At night they camped in a wood beyond the Hacienda del Toro, which building they saw rising gloomy and tranquil like an eagle's nest on the top of its rock, and they passed close to it during the afternoon.

The country assumed a wilder and more abrupt aspect; the grass was thicker, the trees were larger, older, and closer together; it was evident that the travellers were at the extreme limit of civilization, and would soon find themselves in the Red territory, although nominally, at least on the maps, this territory figured among the possessions of the Mexican Confederation. This feature, by the way, is found everywhere throughout the New World. Even in the United States, which pretend, erroneously, we believe, to be more civilized than their neighbours, towns with high-flown names may be seen on the maps of their large possessions, which only exist in reality as a name painted on a solitary post, planted in the centre of a plain or on the bank of a river, without even a keeper to watch over the preservation of this post, which, worn by wind and sun, eventually disappears, though the town never sprung up in its place. During our travels we were too often the victim of this humorous Yankee mystification not to feel angry with this eccentric nation, which repeats to every new comer that it marches at the head of civilization, and has a mission to regenerate the New World.

The two men, after lighting their watch-fire, supped with good appetite, rolled themselves in their zarapes and fell asleep, trusting to the instinct of their horses to warn them of the approach of any enemy, whether man or wild beast, that attempted to surprise them during their slumbers. But nothing disturbed them; the night was quiet; at sunrise they awoke, mounted, and continued their journey, which would only take a few hours longer.

"I am mistaken," the hunter said suddenly, turning to his companion.

"How so?" the latter asked.

"Because," Stronghand replied, "I told you yesterday we should not reach the *atepetl* till the afternoon."

"Well?"

"We shall be there by eleven o'clock."

"*Caramba!* That is famous news."

"When we have crossed that hill we shall see the village a short distance a-head of us, picturesquely grouped on the side of another hill, and running into the plain, where the last houses are built on the banks of a pretty little stream, whose white and limpid waters serve as a natural rampart."

"Tell me, comrade, what do you think of the reception that will be offered us?"

"The Papazos are hospitable."

"I do not doubt it; unluckily, I have no claims to the kindness of the Red-skins. Moreover, I know that they are very suspicious, and never like to see white men enter their villages."

"That depends on the way in which white men try to enter them."

"There is another reason which, I confess, supplies me with reason for grave thought."

"What is it?"

"It is said—mark me, I do not assert it——"

"All right; go on."

"It is said that the Papazos are excited, and on the point of revolting, if they have not done so already."

"They rose in insurrection some days ago," Stronghand coolly answered.

"What?" the majordomo exclaimed, greatly startled, "and you are leading me to them?"

"Why not?"

"Because we shall be massacred, that's all."

The hunter shrugged his shoulders.

"You are mad."

"I am mad—I am mad!" Paredes repeated, shaking his head very dubiously; "it pleases you to say that, but I am not at all desirous, if I can avoid it, of thus placing myself in the power of men who must be my enemies."

"I repeat that nothing will happen to you. *Viva Dios!* do you fancy me capable of leading you into a snare?"

"No; on my honour that is not my thought; but you may be mistaken, and credit these savages with feelings they do not possess."

"I am certain of what I assert. Not only have you nothing to fear, but you will have an honourable reception."

"Honourable?" the majordomo remarked, with an air of incredulity; "I am not very certain of that."

"You shall see. Woe to the man who dared to hurt a hair of your head while you are in my company."

"Who are you, to speak thus?"

"A hunter, nothing else; but I am a friend of the Papazos, and adopted son of one of their tribes; and every man, though he were the mortal enemy of the nation, must, for my sake, be received as a brother by the sachems and warriors."

"Well, be it so," the majordomo muttered, in the tone of a man forced in his last entrenchments, and who resolves to make up his mind.

"Besides," the hunter added, "any hesitation would now be useless, and perhaps dangerous."

"Why so?"

"Because the Indians have their scouts scattered through the woods and over the plain already; they saw and signalled our approach long ago, and if we attempted to turn back, it would justly appear suspicious; and then we should suddenly see Indians rise all round us, and be immediately made prisoners, before we even thought of defending ourselves."

"*Demonio!* that makes the matter singular, comrade; then you believe we have been seen already?"

"Would you like to have a proof on the spot?" the hunter asked, laughingly.

"Well, I should not mind, for I should then know what I have to expect."

"Well, I will give you the proof."

The travellers had reached the foot of the hill, and were at this moment concealed by the tall grass that surrounded them. Stronghand stopped his horse, and imitated the cry of the mawkawis twice. Almost immediately the grass parted, an Indian bounded from a thick clump of trees with the lightness of an antelope, and stopped two yards from the hunter, on whom he fixed his black, intelligent eyes, without saying a word. The apparition of the Red-skin was so sudden, his arrival so unexpected, that, in spite of himself, the majordomo could not restrain a start of surprise.

This Indian was a man of three-and-twenty years of age at the most, whose exquisite proportions made him resemble a statue of Florentine bronze; the whole upper part of his body was naked; his unloosened hair hung in disorder over his shoulders; his clothing merely consisted of trousers sewn with horsehair, fastened round the loins by a belt of untanned leather, and tied at the ankles. A tomahawk and a scalping-knife—weapons which the Indians never lay aside—hung from his belt, and he leant with careless grace upon a long rifle of American manufacture. The hunter bowed, and after stretching out his arm, with the palm turned down and the fingers straight, said, in a gentle voice—

"Wah! the Wacondah protects me, since the first person I see, on returning to my people, is Sparrow Hawk."

The young Indian bowed in his turn with the native courtesy characteristic of the Red-skin, and replied in a guttural voice, which, however, was very gentle—

"For a long time the sachems have been informed of the coming of the Great Bear of their Nation; they thought that only one chief was worthy saluting Stronghand on his return. Sparrow Hawk is happy that he was chosen by them."

"I thank the sachems of my nation," the hunter said, with a meaning glance at the majordomo, "for having deigned to do me so signal an honour. Will my son return to the village with us, or will he precede us?"

"Sparrow Hawk will go ahead, in order that the guest of Stronghand, my father, may be received with the honours due to a man who comes in the company of the Great Bear."

"Good! my brother will act as becomes a chief. Stronghand will not detain him longer."

The young Indian bowed his head in assent, leapt backwards, and disappeared in the thicket whence he had emerged, with such rapidity, that if the grass had not continued to undulate after his departure, his apparition would have seemed like a dream.

"We can now start again," the hunter said to the majordomo, who was utterly confounded.

"Let us go!" the latter answered, mechanically.

"Well," answered Stronghand, "do you now believe that you have anything to fear among the Papazos?"

"Excuse me; as you said, I was a madman to fear it."

They crossed the plain, following a wild-beast track which, after numberless windings, reached a ford, and in about an hour they arrived at the bank of the river. Twelve Papazo Indians, dressed in their war-paint and mounted on magnificent horses, were standing motionless and in single file in front of the ford. So soon as they perceived the two travellers, they uttered loud shouts and dashed forward to meet them, firing their guns, brandishing their weapons, and waving their white female buffalo robes, which, by-the-bye, only the most renowned sachems of the nation have the right to wear. The two white men, on their side, spurred their horses, responding to the shouts of the Indians, and firing their guns. All at once, at a signal from one of the chiefs, all the horsemen stopped, and arranged themselves round the travellers, to act as an escort. The whole party crossed the ford and entered the village, amid the deafening shouts of the women and children, with which were inharmoniously blended the bark of dogs, the hoarse notes of the shells, and the shrill sounds of the *chichikouès*.

CHAPTER XVI.

THE ATEPETL.

MANY persons imagine that all Indians are alike, and that the man acquainted with the manners of one tribe knows them all. This is a serious error, which it is important to dissipate. Among the Indians, properly so called—that is to say, the aborigines of America—will be found as many differences in language, dialect, &c., as among the nations of the Old Continent, if not more. The number of dialects spoken by the Indians is infinite; the manners of one nation form a complete contrast with those of another living only a few leagues away; and any person who, after travelling for some time in the Far West, asserted that he was thoroughly acquainted with the character of the Indians and their mode of life, would be quite deceived; and more serious still, would deceive those whom he pretended to instruct.

The Indians are divided into two great families: the cultivating Indians—that is to say, those who are sedentary and attached to the soil they till; and hunter or nomadic Indians, who have a great resemblance to the Touaricks of Africa and the Tartars of Asia. The hunting Indians, known as *Indios Bravos,* inhabit leathern huts, easy of transport from one place to another, and only remain stationary so long as the country supplies them with the necessary forage for their horses and the game indispensable for the men. The tame Indians, or *Indios Mansos,* on the other hand, are permanently established at a carefully-selected spot; they have built actual houses, in which they shelter themselves and keep their winter provisions. These Indians, though they follow the customs of their fathers, recognise the Mexican laws, obey them ostensibly, are apparent Christians, though they secretly practise all the rites of their old faith; and their chief assumes the title of Alcalde. In a word, they are nearly as much civilized as the majority of the creoles.

The confederation of the Papazos was composed of several nations, combining both Indios Mansos and Indios Bravos. The latter, though harmless, and consequently nomadic, had, in the heart of unexplored forests or the gorges of the Sierra Madre, their winter villages—a collection of huts made of branches and covered with mud, where in the event of war their squaws found refuge, and which served them, after an expedition, to hide the plunder they had made.

The Gilenos, whose powerful nation was composed of one hundred and eighteen distinct tribes, each of which had its private totem or standard, formed the principal branch of the Confederation of the Papazos. The Gilenos are essentially agricultural. At a period which it would be impossible to state with certainty, because the Indians do not write anything down, but trust to tradition, the Comanche nation, which proudly calls itself the "Queen of the Prairies," and asserts, perhaps justly, that it is descended in a straight line from the Chichimeques, the first conquerors of Mexico, was divided into two parts after a council held by the chiefs, for the sake of terminating a dispute that threatened to degenerate into a civil war. One half the nation continued to wander in the immense prairies of the Far West, and retained the name of Comanche. The other tribes settled on the banks of the Rio Gila, gave up hunting for agriculture, while retaining their independence, and only nominally obeying the Spaniards and Mexicans. Eventually they received the name of Gilenos, from the river on whose banks they originally settled. But, although separated, the two divisions of the Comanche nation continued to maintain friendly relations, recognised each other as springing from the same stem, and helping one another whenever circumstances demanded it.

The Gilenos piously preserved the faith of their fathers, maintained their customs; among others that of never drinking spirituous liquors; and never permitted the Mexican Government to establish among them that system of annoyance and rapine under which it mercilessly bows the other Indian mansos. The Gileno villages are distinguished from all the others by their singular construction, which admirably displays the character of this people. We will attempt to convey an idea of them to the reader.

Stronghand had pointed out to the major-domo clusters of storied houses, suspended as it were from the flank of the hill. But these houses were only built temporarily, and in case of an attack on the village would be immediately destroyed. The hill, doubtless in consequence of one of those natural convulsions so common in these regions, was separated into two parts by a quebrada of enormous depth, which served as the bed of an impetuous torrent. On either side of this quebrada the Indians had built an enormous construction of pyramidal shape, upwards of two hundred and fifty feet in height. These two towers contained the lodgings of the inhabitants, their granaries and storehouses. More than eight hundred beings, men, women, and children, resided in these singular buildings, which were connected together at the top by a bridge of llianas, boldly thrown across the abyss. These towers could only be entered by a ladder, which was drawn up each night; for as a last and essential precaution, the doors were sixty feet from the ground, in order to guard against surprise.

Nothing could be more curious or picturesque than the appearance offered at a distance by this strange village, with its two massive towers, having ladders for stairs, up and down which people were constantly moving. A few days previously, for greater safety, and to guard the village from a surprise, the chiefs had a trench dug, and a palisade erected composed of stakes fastened together by llianas. The Indians had taken this precaution to prevent their horses, on which they especially calculated for the success of the meditated expedition, being carried off by surprise, as so frequently happens on the border.

The travellers were conducted with great ceremony by the chiefs who had come to receive them at the entrance of the village to the square, on one side of which stood the "Ark of the First Man;" on the other, "The Great Medicine Lodge, or Council Hut." During the ride the majordomo fancied he saw among the crowd several individuals belonging to the white race, and mentioned it to his comrade.

"You are not mistaken," the latter replied; "several Mexicans reside in the village and trade with the Indians; but that must not surprise you, for you are aware that the Gilenos are mansos. Stay, here is a monk."

In fact, at this moment a stout, rubicund monk crossed the square, distributing blessings right and left, of which the Indians seemed to take but little notice.

"These worthy Frayles," the hunter continued, "lead here a rather monastic life, but in spite of the trouble they take they cannot succeed in making proselytes. The Comanches are too attached to their religion to accept another; still, as they are too savage to be intolerant," he added, ironically, "they allow these poor monks entire liberty on the express condition that they do not interfere with them. They have even permitted them to build a chapel, a very poor and simple edifice, in which a few passing adventurers offer up their prayers; for the inhabitants of the village never set foot in it."

"I will go to it," said Paredes.

"And you will act rightly. However, I will do this justice to the four monks who, through a love of proselytism, have confined themselves to this forgotten nook, of stating that they bear an excellent reputation, do all the good they can, and are generally beloved and respected by the population. This praise is the more valuable because the Mexican clergy do not enjoy a great reputation for sanctity."

"But now that war is declared, what will become of these monks?"

"What do you think? They will remain peacefully without fearing insult or annoyance. However savage the Indians may be, they are not so savage, be assured, as to make the innocent suffer for the crimes of the guilty."

"Forgive me, Stronghand, if I remark that I notice with sorrow, in your mode of expressing yourself, a certain bitterness which seems to me unjust. The secret sympathies of an honest man ought not, in any case, to render him partial."

"I allow that I am wrong, my friend. When you know me better, you will be indulgent, I doubt not, to this bitterness which I frequently unconsciously display in my language. But here we are at the square, and other more urgent matters claim all our attention."

The plaza, which the travellers now reached, formed a parallelogram, and rose with a gentle ascent to the foot of the tower on the left of the village. Several streets opened into it, and the houses built on either side of it had an appearance of cleanliness and comfort which is but rarely found in Indian villages; and if this pueblo had been inhabited by white Creoles, it would certainly have obtained the title of *ciudad.* In front of the council-lodge stood three men, whom it was easy to recognise as the principal chiefs of the village by their hats of racoon skin, surrounded by a gold golilla, and the silver-mounted cane, like that of our beadles, which they held in their right hand. The Mexicans, among other customs they took from the Spaniards, have retained that of investing the Indian chiefs with authority. This investiture, generally performed by a delegate of the governor of the province, consists in giving them the hat and stick to which we have referred. These three chiefs, therefore, ostensibly held their power from the Mexican government, but in reality the latter had only obeyed the feudal claims of the tribes assembled at this village, by conferring the authority on these men whom their countrymen had long previously recognised as chiefs.

The procession halted before the alcaldes, or, to use the Indian term, the sachems. The latter were men of a ripe age, with a haughty and imposing mien. The eldest of them, who stood in the centre, had in his look and the expression of his features something indescribably majestic. He appeared about sixty years of age; a long white beard fell in snowy flakes on his chest; his tall form, his broad forehead, his black eyes, and his slightly aquiline nose, rendered him a very remarkable man. He did not wear the Indian costume, but that adopted by the hunters and woodrangers; a blue cotton shirt fastened round his hips by a leather girdle, which held his arms and ammunition, wide *calzoneras* of deer-hide buckled below the knee, and heavy boots, whose heels were armed with formidable spurs, the wheel of which was as large as a saucer.

In conclusion, the personage we have attempted to describe did not belong to the Indian race, as could be seen at the first glance; but in addition, the fine, elegant, nervous type of the pure Spanish race could be noticed in him. The majordomo could not check a start of surprise at the sight of this man, whose presence seemed to him incomprehensible at such a place and among such people. He leant over to Stronghand, and asked him, in a low voice, choked by involuntary emotion,—

"Who is that man?"

"You can see," the hunter replied, drily, "he is the Alcalde Mayor of the pueblo. But silence! the persons surrounding us are surprised to see us conversing in whispers."

Paredes held his tongue, though his eyes were obstinately fixed on the man to whom the hunter had ironically given the title of Alcalde Mayor. A little to the rear of the chiefs, a warrior was holding the totem of the tribe, representing a condor, the sacred bird of the Incas. A crowd of Indians of both sexes, nearly all armed, filled the square, and pressed forward to witness a scene which was not without a certain grandeur. So soon as the procession halted, Sparrowhawk dismounted and walked up to the sachems.

"Fathers of my nation," he said, "the Great Bear of our tribe has returned, bringing with him a pale-face, his friend."

"He is welcome," the three chiefs answered, unanimously, "as well as his friend, whoever he may be; so long as he pleases to remain among us he will be regarded as a brother."

The hunter then advanced, and bowed respectfully to the sachems.

"Thanks for myself and friend," he said; "the journey we have made was long, and we are worn with fatigue. May we be permitted to take a few hours' rest?"

The Indians were astonished to hear the hunter, a man of iron power, whose reputation for vigour was well established among them, speak of the fatigue he felt. But understanding that he had secret reasons for asking this, no one made a remark.

"Stronghand and his friend are at liberty to proceed to the calli prepared for them," one of the chiefs answered: "Sparrowhawk will guide them."

The two adventurers bowed respectfully, and, preceded by Sparrowhawk, passed through the crowd, which opened before them, and proceeded to the calli appointed for them. Let us state at once that this calli was the property of Stronghand, who inhabited it whenever business or accident brought him to the village. By the order of the chiefs, however, it had been prepared for the reception of two persons. So soon as the travellers reached the calli, Sparrow-hawk retired, after whispering a few words in the ear of the hunter. The latter replied by a sign of assent, and then turned to the majordomo, who was already engaged in unsaddling his horse.

"You are at home, comrade," he said to him; "use this house as you think proper. I have to see a person to whom I will introduce you presently. I will, therefore, leave you for the present, but I shall not be absent long."

And without awaiting an answer, the hunter turned his horse, and started at a gallop.

"Hum!" the Mexican muttered, so soon as he was alone, "all this is not clear; did I do wrong in trusting to this man? I will be on my guard."

CHAPTER XVII.

THE SPY.

After installing the majordomo in the calli, Stronghand proceeded through the village, taking an apparently careless glance around, but in reality not letting anything unusual escape his notice. The Indians whom the hunter met addressed him as an old acquaintance; the very women and children tried to attract his attention by their hearty bursts of laughter and their greetings of welcome. For all and for each the hunter had a pleasant remark, and thus satisfied the frequently indiscreet claims of those who pressed around him. Thus accompanied, he went right through the village, and, on reaching the foot of the left-hand pyramid, dismounted, threw his horse's bridle to a boy, bidding him lead the horse to his calli, and forced his way with some difficulty through the crowd, whose curiosity seemed to increase instead of diminishing. He walked up to the ladder, and after waving his hand to the Indians, hurried up it, and disappeared inside the pyramid.

This strange building, which was almost shapeless outside, was internally arranged with the utmost care and most perfect intelligence. The hunter, who was doubtless anxious to reach his destination, only took a hurried glance at the rooms he passed through; he went up an internal staircase, and soon reached the top of the pyramid. Sparrowhawk was standing motionless before a cougar's skin hung up in lieu of a door, and on seeing the hunter he bowed courteously.

"My father has not delayed," he said, with a good-tempered smile.

"Has the council begun yet?" Stronghand asked.

"For four suns the elders of the nation have remained without taking rest round the council fire; the arrival of my father was alone able to make them suspend their labours for an hour."

The hunter frowned.

"Cannot I speak to the great sachem for a moment?"

"I cannot give my father any information on that point."

"Good!" the hunter continued, apparently forming a determination. "Has Sparrowhawk no instructions for me?"

"None but to await Stronghand, and announce his arrival."

"Wah! here I am; my brother's instructions are fulfilled."

Without replying, Sparrowhawk raised the curtain, and allowed the hunter to pass into the council-hall.

In a large room, which was entirely destitute of furniture—unless that name can be given to dried buffalo skulls employed as seats—some twenty persons were gravely seated in a circle, smoking a calumet silently, whose mouthpiece constantly passed from hand to hand. In the centre of the circle was a golden brasier, in which burned the sacred fire of Moctecuzoma, a fire which must never go out. According to tradition, the last Emperor of Mexico shared it among his dearest partisans on the eve of his death; and this fire, it is also said, derives its origin from the sun itself.

The presence of this fire in the room, which was generally kept in a subterraneous vault, inaccessible to the sight of the common herd, and which is only shown to the people on grand occasions, proved the gravity of the matters the council had to discuss. Moreover, the appearance of the chiefs assembled in the room had about it something stern and imposing that inspired respect. Contrary to Indian habits, they were all unarmed. This precaution, which was owing to the advice of the principal sachem of the nation, was justified not only by the considerable number of chiefs present, but also by their belonging to various nations. Each tribe of the grand confederation of the Papazos had its representative in this assembly, where were also the sachems of nations ordinarily at war with it, but who, in the hope of a general revolt against the whites, the implacable enemies of the red race, had forgotten their hatred for a season. Here could be seen Yaquis, Mayos, Seris, and even free hunters and trappers, white and half-bred, in their grand war paint, with their heels adorned with wolves' tails, an honorary distinction to which only the great braves have a right.

Thunderbolt, the old man whose portrait we have just drawn, presided over the assembly. On the entrance of Stronghand, all the warriors rose, turned to him, and after bowing gracefully, invited him to take a seat among them. The hunter, flattered in his heart by the honour done him, bowed gravely to the members of the council, and seated himself on the right of Thunderbolt, after handing his weapons to Sparrowhawk, who carried them into an adjoining room. There was a rather long silence, during which the hunter smoked the calumet which had been eagerly offered him. At length Thunderbolt began speaking.

"My son could not arrive at a better moment," he said, addressing Stronghand; "his return was eagerly desired by his brothers. He has come from the country inhabited by our enemies; without doubt he will give us news."

The hunter rose, looked round the meeting, and replied—

"I have been among the Gachupinos, I have entered their towns, I have seen their pueblos, presidios, and posts; like ourselves, they are preparing for war; they understand the extent of the danger that threatens them, and are trying to neutralize it by all means."

"The news is not very explicit; we hoped that Stronghand would give us more serious information about the movements of the enemy," Thunderbolt remarked, with a reproachful accent.

"Perhaps I could do so," the hunter replied, calmly.

"Then why are you silent?"

The young man hesitated for a moment beneath the glances fixed on him.

"The white men have a proverb," he said, at length, "whose justice I specially recognise at this moment."

"What is it?"

"Words are silver, but silence is gold."

"Which means?" Thunderbolt continued, eagerly.

"The most formidable weapon of the white man is treachery," the hunter continued, not appearing to heed the interruption; "they have even conquered by treachery the Red-skins, whom they did not dare meet face to face. Questions so interesting as those we have to settle, such serious interests as we have to discuss, must not be treated in so large an assembly ere it is quite certain that a traitor has not glided in among us. So long as merely general questions are discussed this is of slight consequence; but so soon as we discuss the means to be employed in carrying on the war, it is urgent that the enemy should not be warned of the result of our deliberations.

"We cannot act otherwise than we are doing. Yes, and that is why the whites are cleverer than we: so soon as war is declared, they appoint a commission, composed of three members, or five at the most, who have to draw up the plan of the campaign. Why do we not do the same? Nothing is more simple, it seems to me: choose, among the chiefs assembled here, a certain number of wise men accustomed to command; these men will assemble in secret, and decide on the means to be employed in conquering our enemy: in this way, if the Spaniards are informed of our movements, the traitor cannot escape us for long. The other chiefs, and the deputies of the friendly natives and confederated tribes, will settle in the Grand Council the common interests of the Indian natives, and the terms to be established among them, in order to stifle for ever those germs of discord which frequently spring up from a misunderstanding, and almost always degenerate into sanguinary and interminable quarrels. I have spoken: my brothers will determine whether my words deserve being taken into consideration."

After bowing to the audience, the hunter sat down again, and seemed to be plunged into deep thought. One of the instinctive qualities of the Indian race is good sense. The chiefs, in spite of the circumlocution in which the hunter had thought it necessary to envelop his remarks, had perfectly understood him: they had caught the justice of his reasoning, and the advantage of a speedy decision on a subject so interesting to the entire confederation: they guessed, under the hunter's reticence, a name which, for secret reasons of his own, he did not wish to utter, and hence his speech was greeted with a buzz of satisfaction, which is always flattering to the ears of an orator, no matter the nature of his hearers. Thunderbolt questioned the members of the council by a glance; all replied with an affirmative shake of their heads.

"Your plan is adopted," the chief said; "we recognise the necessity of carrying it out. But this time again we must apply to you to choose the members of the council whom we have to elect."

"Chance alone must decide the solution. All the sachems collected in this hall are great braves of their tribes, and the picked warriors of their nations. No matter on whom the lot falls, the members will behave honourably in the new council."

"Stronghand has spoken well, as he always does, when he is called upon to give his opinion in the council of the chiefs; now let him finish what he has so well begun, by instructing us of the way in which we are to consult chance."

"Be it so: I will obey my father."

The hunter rose and left the hall, but his absence lasted only a few minutes. During this interval the chiefs remained motionless and silent. Stronghand soon returned, followed by Sparrowhawk, who, as he had been ordered by the sachems to keep the door, had not taken part in the deliberations, though he had a right to do so. This chief carried a blanket tied up so as to form a bag.

"In this blanket," the hunter then said, "I have placed a number of bullets equal to that of the chiefs assembled in council: I have taken these bullets from the ammunition-bag of every one of the chiefs. I have noticed that our guns are of different bores, and hence some of the bullets are larger, others smaller. Each of us will draw a bullet haphazard; when all have one, they will be examined; and the three chiefs, if you fix on that number, or the five, if you prefer that number, to whom chance has given the largest bullets, will compose the new council."

"That is a simple way, and will prevent any annoyance," Thunderbolt said; "I believe that we shall do well by adopting it."

The chiefs bowed their assent.

"But," the sachem continued, "before we begin drawing, let us first settle of how many members the council shall consist; shall there be three or five?"

A white trapper rose and asked leave to speak. It was a man of about forty years of age, with frank and energetic features and muscular limbs, well known all over the western prairies by the singular name of the Whistler.

"If I may be allowed," he said, "to offer my opinion on such a matter before wise men and renowned warriors—for I am only a poor rogue of a hunter—I would call your attention to the fact that, with a committee whose duties are so serious, three men are not sufficient to discuss a question advantageously, because it is so easy to obtain a majority. On the other hand, five men mutually enlighten each other, by exchanging their ideas and starting objections: hence, I am of opinion that the council ought to be composed of five members. I will add one word: Will the white and half-breed hunters and trappers here present take part in the election?"

"Do they not fight with us?" Thunderbolt asked.

"This is true," the Whistler continued; "still it would be, perhaps, better for you to settle the matter among yourselves; we are, in reality, only your allies."

"You are our brothers and friends; in the name of the chiefs of the confederation, I thank you, Whistler, for the delicate proposal you have made; but we do not accept your offer, for all must be in common between you and us."

"You will do as you please. I spoke for your good; and if it does not suit you, say no more about it."

While these remarks were exchanged between the trapper and Thunderbolt, the chiefs had decided that the military commission should be composed of five members. The drawing at once began; each warrior went, in his turn, to draw a bullet from the bag held by Sparrowhawk; then the verification was begun with that good faith and impartiality which the Indians display in all their actions when dealing with one another. On this occasion chance was intelligent, as happens more frequently than is supposed, when it is left free to act: the chiefs chosen to form the committee were exactly those who, if another mode of election had been employed, would have gained all the votes through their talent, experience, and wisdom. Hence, the sachems frankly applauded the decision of fate, and in their superstition, derived from this caprice of accident a favourable augury for the result of the war. The committee was composed as follows:—

Thunderbolt, Sparrowhawk, Stronghand, the Whistler, and a renowned Apache chief, whose name was the Peccary.

When the election was over, just as the chiefs were returning to their seats, Stronghand approached a trapper, who, ever since his entrance, had seemed to shun his eye, and conceal himself, as far as possible, behind the other chiefs. Tapping him on the shoulder, he said in a low but imperative voice—

"Master Kidd, two words, if you please."

The adventurer, for it was really he, started at the touch, but immediately recovering himself, he turned his smiling face to the hunter's, and said, with a respectful bow—

"I am quite at your service, caballero; can I be so happy as to be able to help you in anything?"

"Yes," the hunter answered, drily.

"Speak, caballero, speak; and as far as lies in my power——"

"A truce to these hypocritical protestations," Stronghand rudely interrupted him, "and let us come to facts."

"I am listening to you," the other said, trying to hide his anxiety.

"This is the point—rightly or wrongly, your presence here offends me."

"What can I do to prevent that, my dear senor?"

"A very simple thing."

"What is it, if you please?"

"Leave the tower at once, mount your horse, and be off."

"Oh!" the bandit said, with a forced laugh, "allow me to remark, my dear senor, that the idea seems to me a singular one."

"Do you think so?" the hunter remarked, coldly; "well, opinions differ. For my part, I consider it quite natural."

"Of course you are jesting."

"Do you fancy me capable of jesting—before all, with a man like you? I think not. Well, I repeat, be off; be off as quickly as possible. I advise you for your own good."

"I must have an excuse for such a flight. What will the Indian chiefs who did me the honour of summoning me to their grand council, and my friends the hunters, suppose, on seeing me thus abandon them without any apparent motive, at the very moment when the war is about to begin?"

"That does not concern me; I want you to be off at once; if not——"

"Well?"

"I shall blow out your brains in the presence of all as a traitor and a spy. You understand me now, my master, I think?"

The bandit started violently; his face became livid, and for some minutes he fixed his viper eye on the hunter, who examined him ironically; then bending down to his ear, he said, in a voice choked with rage and shame, "Stronghand, you are the stronger, and any resistance on my part would be mad; I shall go, therefore; but remember this, I shall be avenged."

Stronghand shrugged his shoulders contemptuously. "Do so," he said, "if you can; but, in the meanwhile, be off if you do not wish me to carry out my threat!" and he turned his back on the bandit. Kidd gave him a parting look of fury, and without adding a word, left the hall. Ten minutes later he was galloping on the road to the Real de Minas, revolving the most sinister schemes.

CHAPTER XVIII.

THE COUNCIL OF THE SACHEMS.

ALTHOUGH the chiefs had guessed from Stronghand's gestures what was going on between him and the American bandit, not one of them made the slightest allusion to Kidd's departure, or even seemed to notice it. The Canadian trapper, named Whistler, alone went up to the hunter, and pressing his hand, said, with a coarse laugh—

"By heavens! comrade, you did not miss your game, but brought it down at the first shot. Receive my sincere congratulations for having freed us of that skunk, who is neither fish nor flesh, and whose roguish face did not at all please me."

"It would please you much less, my good fellow, if you knew him," the hunter replied, with a smile.

"I beg you to believe that I have no

desire to form a closer acquaintance with that picaro; only too many like him may be met on the prairies."

The chiefs had resumed their seats, and the council, which had been momentarily interrupted, was reopened by Thunderbolt. The Indians, though people think proper to regard them as savages, could give lessons in urbanity and good breeding to the members of parliamentary assemblies in old Europe. Among them a speaker is never interrupted by those coarse and inopportune noises for which some M.P.'s seem to possess a privilege. Each speaks in his turn. The speakers, who are listened to with a religious silence, have the liberty of expressing their ideas without fearing personalities, which are frequently offensive. When the debate is closed, the speaker—that is to say, the oldest chief, or the one of the highest position, either through bravery or wisdom—sums up the discussion in a few words, takes the opinion of the other chiefs, who vote by nodding their heads, and the minority always accepts, without complaint or recrimination of any sort, the resolution of the majority.

Before going further, we will explain, in

a few words, the cause of the dissatisfaction which had induced the Indians to revolt once again against the whites. At the period of the Spanish conquest, the Indians, in spite of the obstinate assertions to the contrary, were happy, or at any rate were, through the intelligent care of the Government, placed in a situation which insured their existence under very satisfactory conditions. It is indubitable that if Spain had retained her colonies for fifty or sixty years longer, she would have gradually succeeded in converting the aborigines of her vast territories, attaching them to the cultivation of the soil, and making them give up a nomadic existence, and adopt the far preferable life in villages.

All Spanish America, both North and South, was covered with missions; that is to say, agricultural colonies, established on a large scale; where monks, in every way respectable, through their complete abnegation of the enjoyments of the world, and their inexhaustible charity, taught the Indians not only the paternal precepts of the Gospel, and their duty to their neighbour, but preaching by example, they became weavers, labourers, cobblers, and blacksmiths, in order to make their docile apprentices more easily understand the way to set to work. These missions contained, at the time of the War of Independence, several hundred thousand Indians, who had given up their nomadic life of hunting, and patiently assumed the yoke of civilization. This magnificent result, obtained by courage and perseverance, and which would have speedily resulted in the solution of a problem declared to be insoluble—the emancipation of the red race, and its aptitude to assume the sedentary condition of a town life, was unhappily not carried further.

When the Mexicans had proclaimed their independence, their first care was to destroy all that the Spaniards had raised, and utterly overthrow the internal governmental system established by them. Naturally, the missions were not exempted from this general overthrow; they were perhaps more kindly treated than the institutions created by the old oppressors. The philosophic spirit of the eighteenth century, when it forced its way into Mexico, was naturally misunderstood and ill appreciated by men who were plunged into the grossest ignorance, and who believed that they displayed the independence and nobility of their character by deadly hatred of the clergy, and abolishing their prerogatives at one stroke. It is true that, by an inevitable reaction, the Mexicans, whose revolution was almost entirely effected by priests, and who, at the outset, displayed themselves as such daring sceptics, ere long fell again, through their superstition, beneath the power of the same clergy, and became more devoted slaves to them than ever.

Unfortunately, the death-blow had been dealt to the missions or agricultural colonies, although the Government recognised its mistake, and sought by all means to palliate it. They never recovered, only languished, and eventually the majority of them fell into ruin, and were utterly abandoned by the Indians, who returned to that desert life from which they had been drawn with such difficulty. Nothing is so heartrending as the sight now offered by these missions, which were once so rich, so full of life, and so flourishing; only a few Indians can be seen, wandering about like ghosts in the deserted cloisters, led by an old white-haired monk, whom they would not leave, and who had vowed to die among his children.

The Mexican Government did not stop

here. Returning to the old errors of the conquistadors, it grew accustomed to regard the Indians as slaves; imposing on them exorbitant tariffs for articles of primary necessity, which it sold to them through special agents, bowing them to any Draconian law, and carrying their injustice so far as to deny them intellect, and brand them with the name of *Gente sin razon*, or people without reason. The consequences of such a system can be easily comprehended. The Indians, who, at the outset, contented themselves with passively withdrawing, and seeking in the desert the liberty that was refused them, on finding themselves so unjustly treated, and urged to desperation by such insults, thought about avenging themselves, and requiting evil for evil.

Then recommenced those periodical invasions of the Indian borders which the Spaniards had repressed with such difficulty and such bloodshed. Murder and pillage were organized on a grand scale, and with such success, that the Comanches and Apaches, to vex the whites, gave the ironical name of the "Mexican moon" to the month they selected to commit their periodical depredations. The subjected Indians—that is to say, those who, in spite of the constant vexations to which they were victims, remained attached to their villages—revolted several times, and on each occasion the Mexican Government succeeded in making them return to their duty by promises and concessions, which were violated and forgotten so soon as the red-skins had laid down their arms. The war, consequently, became generalized and permanent in the Border states of the confederation.

But with the exception of a few invasions more serious than others, the Indians had almost entirely confined themselves to keeping the whites on the alert, when the great insurrection of 1827 broke out, which all but succeeded in depriving Mexico of her richest provinces. This insurrection was the more terrible, because on this occasion the Indians, guided by experienced chiefs, possessing firearms, and carrying out tactics entirely different from those they had hitherto employed, waged a serious war, and insisted on retaining the provinces they had seized. The red-skins elected an emperor and established a government; they displayed a settled intention of definitively regaining their independence and reconstituting their nationality.

The Mexicans, justly terrified by these manifestations, made the greatest sacrifices in order to quell this formidable revolt, and succeeded, though rather owing to the treachery and disunion they managed to sow among the chiefs than by the power of their arms. But this uprising had caused them to reflect, and they saw that it was high time to come to an arrangement with these men, whom they had hitherto been accustomed to regard as irrational beings. Peace was concluded on conditions very advantageous to the Indians and their forces; and the Mexicans, owing to the fright they had endured, were compelled to keep their promises, or, to speak more correctly, pretended to do so.

For several years the Indians, satisfied with this apparent amelioration in the relations between them and the whites, remained peacefully in their villages, and the Mexicans had only to defend their borders against the attacks of the wild or unsubjected Indians. This was a task, we are bound to confess, in which they were not very successful; for the Indians eventually passed the limits the Spaniards had imposed on them, permanently established themselves on the ruins of the old Creole villages, and by degrees, and gaining ground each year, they reduced the territory of the Mexican Government in an extraordinary way.

Still, when the remembrance of the great Indian insurrection seemed to have died out, and the Indios mansos had apparently accepted the sovereignty of Mexico, the annoyances recommenced. Though at first slight, they gradually became more and more frequent, owing to the apathetic resignation of the Indians, and the patience with which they uncomplainingly endured the unjust aggressions of which they were made the systematic victims. The concessions granted under the pressure of fear were brutally withdrawn, and matters returned to the same state as before the insurrection. The Indians continued to suffer, apparently resigned to endure all the insults it might please their oppressors to make them undergo: but this calm concealed a terrific storm, and the Mexicans would shortly be aroused by a thunder-clap.

The red-skins behaved, under the circumstances, with rare prudence and circumspection, in order not to alarm the persons they wished to surprise. They would certainly have succeeded in deceiving the Mexicans as to their plans, had it not been for the treachery of the agents of the Mexican Government, continually kept in their villages to watch them, among whom was Kidd, whom Stronghand had so suddenly unmasked and contemptuously turned out. Still these agents, in spite of their lively desire to make themselves of importance by magnifying facts, had only been able to give very vague details about the conspiracy the Indians were secretly forming. They knew that an emperor had been elected, and that he was a white man, but they did not know who he was or his name. They also knew that the Confederation of the Papazos had placed itself at the head of the movement, and intended to deal the first blow, but no one was aware when or how hostilities would commence.

This information, however, incomplete though it was, appeared to the Mexicans, on whose minds at once rushed the sanguinary memories of the last revolution, sufficiently serious for them to place themselves in a position to resist the first attack of the red-skins, which is always so terrible, and to place their frontiers in such a state as would prevent a surprise—a thing they had never yet succeeded in effecting. The Mexican Government, warned of what was going on by the commandants of the States of Sonora and Cinaloa, the two most menaced of the Confederation, and recognising the gravity of the case, resolved to send troops from the capital to reinforce the border garrisons. This plan, unfortunately, could not be carried out, and was the cause of fresh and very dangerous complications.

It is only in the old Spanish colonies, which are in the deepest state of neglect and disorganization, that such acts are possible. The troops told off to proceed to Sonora, so soon as they learned that they were intended to oppose the Indians, peremptorily refused to march, alleging as the reason, that they were not at all desirous of fighting savages who did not respect the law of nations, and had no scruples about scalping their prisoners. The president of the republic, strong in his right and the danger the country ran, tried to insist and force them to set out. Then a thing that might be easily foreseen occurred: not only did the troops obstinately remain in revolt, but set the seal on it by making a pronunciamento in favour of the general chosen to command the expedition, and who, we may do him the justice of saying, had been the first to declare against the departure of the troops from the capital.

This pronunciamento was the spark that fired the powder-train. In a few days the whole of Mexico was a prey to the horrors of a civil war; so that the governors of the two States, being reduced to their own forces, and not knowing whether they would retain their posts under the new president, were more embarrassed than ever, did not dare take any initiative, and contented themselves with throwing up such intrenchments as they could, though they had quite enough to do in keeping their troops to their duty, and keeping them from deserting. Such was the state of things at the moment we have now reached. This information, upon which we have purposely laid a stress, in order to make the reader understand certain facts which, without this precaution, would seem to belong rather to the regions of fancy than to that of history, as they are so strange and incredible, was reported by Stronghand to the council of the sachems, and listened to in a religious silence.

"Now," he added, in conclusion, "I believe that the moment has arrived to strike the grand blow for which we have so long been preparing. Our enemies hesitate; they are demoralized; their soldiers tremble; and I am convinced they will not withstand the attack of our and the great Beaver's warriors. This is what I wished to say to the council. Still it was not advisable that such important news should reach the ears of our enemies. The sachems will judge whether I have acted well, or if my zeal carried me too far in dismissing from the council a pale-face who, I am convinced, is a traitor sold to the Mexicans. I have spoken."

A flattering murmur greeted the concluding remarks of the young man, who sat down, blushing.

"It appears to me," Whistler then said, "that the debate need not be a long one. As war is decided on, the council of the Confederation has only to seek allies among the other Indian nations, in order to augment the number of our warriors, if that be possible. As regards the operations, and the period when the Mexican territory is to be invaded, that will devolve on the military committee, who pledge themselves to the profoundest secresy about their discussions, until the hour for action arrives. I have spoken."

Thunderbolt rose.

"Chiefs and sachems of the Confederation of the Papazos," he said, in his sympathetic and sonorous voice, "and you, warriors, our allies, the moment for dissolving your council has at length arrived. Henceforth the committee of the five chiefs will alone sit. Each of you will return to his tribe, arm his warriors, and order the scalp-dance to be performed round the war-post; but the eighth sun must see you here again at the head of your warriors, in order that all may be ready to act when the invasion is decided on. I have spoken. Have I said well, powerful men?"

The chiefs rose in silence, resumed their weapons, and immediately left the village, starting in different directions at a gallop.

Thunderbolt and Stronghand were left alone.

"My son," the old man then said, "have you nothing to tell me?"

"Yes, father," the young man respectfully answered; "I have very serious news for you."

CHAPTER XIX.

THE RANCHO.

Before describing the conversation between Thunderbolt and Stronghand, we are obliged to go back, and tell the reader certain facts which had occurred at the Hacienda del Toro, a few days before the majordomo set out for Hemosillo. Mexican girls, born and bred on the Indian border, enjoy a liberty which the want of society renders indispensable. Always on horseback upon these immense estates, which extend for twenty or five-and-twenty leagues, their life is spent in riding over hill and dale, visiting the wretched huts of the vaqueros and peons, relieving their wants, and rendering themselves beloved by their simple graces and affecting goodness of heart.

Donna Marianna, who had been exiled for several years at a convent, so soon as she returned home, eagerly renewed her long rides through forests and prairies, to see again the persons in her father's employ, with whom she had sported as a child, and of whom she had such a pleasant recollection. At times followed by a servant, specially attached to her, but more usually alone, the maiden had therefore recommenced her rides, going to visit one and the other, enjoying her gallop, careless as a bird, pleased with everything—the flowers she culled as she passed, the reviving breeze she inhaled, and smiling gaily at the sun which bronzed her complexion; in a word, she revealed the voluptuous and egotistic apathy of a child in whom the woman is not yet revealed, and who is ignorant that she possesses a heart.

Most usually Donna Marianna guided her horse to a rancho situated about three leagues from the hacienda, in the midst of a majestic forest of evergreen oaks and larches. This rancho, which was built of adobes, and whitewashed, stood on the bank of a stream, in the centre of a field sufficiently cleared to grow the grain required for the support of the poor inhabitants of the hovel. In the rear of the rancho was an enclosure, serving as a corral, and containing two cows and four or five horses, the sole fortune of the master of this rancho, which, however, internally was not so poverty-stricken as the exterior seemed to forebode. It was divided into three parts, two of which served as bed-rooms, and the third as sitting-room, saloon, kitchen, &c. In the latter, the fowls impudently came to pick up grain and pieces of tortillas which had been allowed to fall.

On the right was a sort of low fireplace, evidently for culinary purposes; the middle of the room was occupied by a large oak table with twisted legs; at the end, two doors opened into the bed-rooms, and the walls were covered with those hideous coloured plates which Parisian trade inundates the New World with, and under which intelligent hawkers print the names of saints, to render the sale more easy. Among these engravings was one representing Napoleon crossing the St. Bernard, accompanied by a guide, holding his horse. It bore the rather too fanciful title, "The great St. Martin dividing his cloak with a beggar." A fact which imparts incomparable meaning to this humorous motto is, that the general, far from wishing to give his cloak to the guide, who does not want it, seems to be shivering with cold, and wrapping himself up with extreme care. Lastly, a few *butaccas* and *equipals* completed the furniture, which, for many reasons, might be considered elegant in a country where the science of comfort is completely ignored, and the wants of material life are reduced to their simplest expression.

This rancho had been for many years inhabited by the same family, who were the last relics of the Indians dwelling here when the country was discovered by the Spaniards. These Indians, who were mansos, and long converted to Christianity, had been old and faithful servants of the Marquises de Moguer, who were always attached to them, and made it a point of honour to heighten their comforts, and give them their protection under all circumstances. Hence the devotion of these worthy people to the Moguer family was affecting, through its simple self-denial. They had forgotten their Indian name, and were only known by that of Sanchez.

At the moment when we introduce this family to the reader, it consisted of three persons: the father, a blind old man, but upright and hale, who, in spite of his infirmity, still traversed all the forest tracks without hesitation or risk of losing himself, merely accompanied by his dog Bouchaley; the mother, a woman of about forty years of age, tall, robust, and possessing marked features, which, when she was younger, must have been very handsome; and the son, a young man of about twenty, well built, and a daring hunter, who held the post of tigrero at the hacienda.

Luisa Sanchez had been nurse to Donna Marianna, and the young lady, deprived at an early age of her mistress, had retained for her not merely that friendship which children generally have for their nurse, and which at times renders the mother jealous, but that craving for affection, so natural in young hearts, and which Donna Marianna, restrained by her father's apparent sternness, could not indulge. The maiden's return to the hacienda caused great joy at the rancho; father, mother, and son at once mounted and proceeded to the Toro to embrace their child, as they simply called her. Halfway they met Donna Marianna, who, in her impatience to see them again, was galloping like a mad girl, followed by her brother, who was teasing her about this love for her nurse.

Since then, not a day passed on which the young lady did not carry the sunshine of her presence to the rancho, and shared the breakfast of the family—a frugal meal, composed of light cakes, roasted on an iron plate, boiled beef seasoned with chile colorado, milk, and *quesadillas*, or cheese-cakes, hard and green and leathery, which the young lady, however, declared to be excellent, and heartily enjoyed. Bouchaley, like everybody else at the rancho, entertained a feeling of adoration for Donna Marianna. He was a long-haired black-and-white mastiff, about ten years old, and spiteful and noisy as all his congeners. In reality, the dog possessed but one good quality—its well-tried fidelity to its master, whom it never took its eyes off, and constantly crouched at his feet. Since the young lady's return, the heart of the worthy quadruped had opened to a new affection; each morning it took its post on the road by which Donna Marianna came, and as soon as it saw her, saluted her by leaps and deafening barks.

Marianno Sanchez, the tigrero, had for his foster-sister an affection heightened by the similarity of name—a similarity which in Spanish America gives a right to a sort of spiritual relationship. This touching custom, whose origin is entirely Indian, is intended to draw closer the relations between *tocayo* and *tocaya*, and they are almost brother and sister. Hence the tigrero, in order to be present each morning at his tocaya's breakfast, often rode eight or ten leagues in the morning, and found his reward in a smile from the young lady. As for Father Sanchez, since the return of his child, as he called her, he only felt one regret. It was that he could not see her and admire her beauty; but he consoled himself by embracing her.

It was about eleven o'clock in the morning; the sun illumined the hut; the birds were singing merrily in the forest. Father Sanchez had taken up the handmill, and was grinding the wheat, while his wife, after sifting the wheat, pounded it and formed it into light cakes, called tortillas, which, after being griddled, would form the solid portion of the breakfast. Bouchaley was at his post on the road, watching for the arrival of the young lady.

"How is it," the old man asked, "that Marianno is not here yet? I generally hear the sound of his horse earlier than this."

"Poor lad! who knows where he is at this moment?" the mother answered. "He has for some days been watching a band of jaguars that have bitten several horses at the hacienda. He is certainly ambushed in some thicket. I only trust he will not be devoured some day by the terrible animals."

"Nonsense, wife," the old man continued, with a shrug of the shoulders. "Maternal love renders you foolish. Marianno devoured by the tigers!"

"Well, I see nothing impossible in that."

"You might just as well say that Bouchaley is capable of chasing a peccari; one thing is as possible as the other. Besides, you forget that our son never goes out without his dog Bigote, a cross between a wolf and a Newfoundland dog, as big as a six-months' old colt, and who is capable of breaking the loins of a coyote at one snap."

"I do not say no, father; I do not say no," she continued, with a shake of her head; "that does not prevent his being a dangerous trade, which may, one day or another, cost him his life."

"Stuff! Mariannо is too clever a hunter for that; besides, the trade is lucrative; each jaguar-skin brings him in fourteen piastres—a sum we cannot afford to despise, since my infirmity has prevented me from working. It would be better for my old carcass to return to the earth, as I am no longer good for anything."

"Do not speak so, father; especially before our daughter, for she would not forgive you: for what you are saying is unjust; you have worked enough in your time to rest now, and your son take your place."

"Well, tell me, wife," the old man said, laughingly, "was I devoured by the jaguar? And yet I was a tigrero for more than forty years, and the jaguars were not nearly so polite in my time as they are now."

"That is all very well; it is true that you have not been devoured, but your father and your grandfather were. What answer have you to that?"

"Hem!" the old man went on, in some embarrassment; "I will answer—I will answer——"

"Nothing, and that will be the best," she continued; "for you could not say anything satisfactory."

"Nonsense! what do you take me for, mother? If my father and grandfather were devoured, and that is true, it was——"

"Well, what? I am anxious to hear."

"Because they were treacherously attacked by the jaguars," he at length said, with a triumphant air; "the wretches knew whom they had to deal with, and so played cunning. Otherwise they would never have got the best of two such clever hunters as my father and grandfather."

The ranchera shrugged her shoulders with a smile, but she considered it unnecessary to answer, as she was well aware she would not succeed in making her husband change his opinion as to her son's dangerous trade. The old man, satisfied with having reduced his wife to silence, as he fancied, did not abuse his victory; with a crafty smile he rolled and lit a cigarette, while Na Luisa laid the table, arranged and dusted everything in the rancho, and listened anxiously to assure herself that the footfall of her son's horse was not mingled with the sounds that incessantly rose from the forest.

All at once Bouchaley was heard barking furiously. The old man drew himself up in his butacca, while Na Sanchez rushed to the doorway, in which Donna Marianna appeared, fresh and smiling.

"Good morning, father! good morning, mother!" she exclaimed in her silvery voice, and kissed the forehead of the old man, who tenderly pressed her to his heart. "Come, Bouchaley, come, be quiet!" she added, patting the dog, which still gambolled round her. "Mother, ask my tocayo to put Negro in the corral, for the good animal has earned its alfalfa."

"I will go, Querida," the old man said; "for to-day I take Marianno's place." And he left the rancho without awaiting an answer.

"Mother," the young lady continued, with a shade of anxiety, "where is my foster-brother? I do not see him."

"Has not arrived yet, nina."

"What! not arrived?"

"Oh, I trust he will soon be here," she said, while stifling a sigh.

The maiden looked at her for a moment sympathetically.

"What is the matter, mother?" she at

length said, as she seized the poor woman's hand; "can any accident have happened?"

"The Lord guard us from it, Querida," Luisa said, clasping her hands.

"Still, you are anxious, mother. You are hiding something from me. Tell me at once what it is."

"Nothing, my child; forgive me. Nothing extraordinary has occurred, and I am hiding nothing from you; but——"

"But what?" Donna Marianna interrupted her.

"Well, since you insist, Querida, I confess to you that I am alarmed. You know that Marianno is tigrero to the hacienda?"

"Yes; what then?"

"I am always frightened lest he should meet with an accident, for that happens so easily."

"Come, come, mother; do not have such thoughts as these. Marianno is an intrepid hunter, and possesses far from common skill and tact."

"Ah, hija, you are of the same opinion as my old man. Alas! if I lost my son, what would become of you?"

"Oh, mother, why talk in that way? Marianno, I hope, runs no danger. The delay that alarms you means nothing; you will soon see him again."

"May you be saying the truth, dear child!"

"I am so convinced of it, mamita, that I will not sit down to table till he arrives."

"Well, you will not have to wait long, hijita," the old man said, as he re-entered the rancho.

"Is he coming?" the mother joyously exclaimed, as she furtively wiped away a tear."

"I knew it," the maiden remarked.

"There, do you hear his horse?" the old man said.

In fact, the furious gallop of a horse echoed in the forest, and approached with the rapidity of a hurricane. The two females darted to the door. At this moment a horseman appeared on the skirt of the clearing, riding at full speed, with his hair floating in the breeze, and his face animated by the speed at which he rode. This horseman, who was powerfully and yet gracefully built, and had a manly, energetic face, was

Marianno, the tigrero. His dog, a black-and-white Newfoundland, with powerful chest and enormous head, was running by the side of the horse, and looking up intelligently every moment.

"Viva Dios! Querida tocaya!" the young man exclaimed, as he leaped from his horse. "I am glad to see you, for I was afraid that I should arrive too late. Bigote," he added, addressing his dog and throwing the bridle to it, which the animal seized with its mouth, "lead Moreno to the corral."

The dog immediately proceeded thither, followed by the horse, while Marianno and the two females returned to the rancho. The young man kissed his father's forehead, and took his hand, saying, "Good morning, papa!" and then returned to his mother, whom he embraced several times.

"Cruel child," she said to him, "why did you delay so long?"

"Pay no attention to what your mother says, muchacho," the old man remarked; "she is foolish."

"Fie! you must not say that!" the young lady exclaimed; "you would do better in scolding Marianno, for I, too, felt alarmed."

"Do not be angry with me," the young man replied; "I have been for some days on the track of a family of jaguars, which is prowling about the neighbourhood, and I could not possibly come sooner."

"Are they about here?"

"No; they are prowlers brought here by the drought; and are the more dangerous because, as they do not belong to these parts, they rest where they please—sometimes at one place, sometimes at another, and it becomes very difficult to follow their trail."

"I only hope they will not think of coming here," the mother said, anxiously.

"I do not believe they will, for wild beasts shun the vicinity of man. Still, Donna Marianna had better, for some days to come, restrict her rides, and not venture too far into the forest."

"What can I have to fear?"

"Nothing, I hope; still it is better to act prudently. Wild beasts are animals whose habits it is very difficult to discover, especially when they are in unknown parts, as these are."

"Nonsense!" the young lady said, with a laugh; "you are trying to frighten me, tocayo."

"Do not believe that; I will accompany you with Bigote to the hacienda."

The dog, which had returned to its master's side after performing its duties, wagged its tail, and looked up in her face.

"I will not allow that, tocayo," the young lady replied, as she passed her hand through the dog's silky coat, and pulled its ears; "let Bigote have a rest. I came alone, and will return alone; and mounted on Negro, I defy the tigers to catch me up, unless they are ambuscaded on my road."

"Still, nina—" Marianno objected.

"Not a word more on the subject, tocayo, I beg; let us breakfast, for I am literally dying of hunger; and were the tigers here," she added, with a laugh, "they might frighten me, but not deprive me of my appetite."

CHAPTER XX.

LOST!

THEY sat down to table; but the meal, in spite of Donna Marianna's efforts to enliven it, suffered from the anxiety which two of the party felt, and tried in vain to conceal. The tigrero was vexed with his foster-sister for not letting him accompany her, for he had not liked to express his fears, lest the young lady on her return to the hacienda might meet the ferocious animals he had been pursuing for some days past, without being able to shoot them.

The jaguar, which is very little known in Europe, is one of the scourges of Mexico, and would figure advantageously in zoological gardens. There is only one in the Parisian Jardin des Plantes, and that is a very small specimen. Let us describe this animal, which is more feared by the Indians and white men of North America, than is the lion by the Arabs. The jaguar (*Felis onca*, or *onza*) is, next to the tiger and lion, the largest of the animals of its genus; it is the great wild cat of Cuvier, and is called indiscriminately "the American tiger," and the "panther of the furriers." It is a quadruped of the feline race; its total length is about nine feet, and its height about twenty-seven inches. Its skin is handsome, and in great request; while of a bright tawny hue on the back, it is marked on the head, neck, and along the flanks with black spots: the lower part of the body is white, with irregular black spots.

But few animals escape the pursuit of the jaguar; it obstinately hunts horses, bulls, and buffaloes; it does not hesitate to leap into rivers to catch certain fish it is fond of, fights the alligator, devours otters and picas, and wages a cruel warfare with the monkeys, owing to its agility, which enables it to mount to the top of trees, even when they are devoid of branches, and upwards of eighty feet high. Although, like all the carnivora of the New World, it shuns the proximity of man, it does not hesitate to attack him when urged by hunger or tracked by hunters; in such cases it fights with the utmost bravery, and does not dream of flight.

Such were the animals the tigrero had been pursuing for the last few days, and had not been able to catch up. According to the sign he had found, the jaguars were four in number—the male, female, and two cubs. We can now understand what the young man's terror must be on thinking of the terrible dangers to which his foster-sister ran a risk of being exposed on her return to the hacienda; but he knew Donna Marianna too well to hope he could make her recal her decision. Hence, he did not try to bring the conversation back to the subject, but resolved to follow her at a distance, in order to come to her aid if circumstances required it.

As always happens under such circumstances, Donna Marianna, seeing that no one referred again to the jaguars, was the first to talk about them, asking her foster-brother the details of their appearance in the country, and the mischief they had done, in what way he meant to surprise them, and a multitude of other questions; to which the young man replied most politely, but limiting himself to brief answers, and without launching into details, which are generally so agreeable to a hunter. The tigrero displayed such laconism in the information he gave the young lady, that the latter, vexed in spite of herself at seeing him so cold upon a subject to which he had seemed to attach such importance a few moments before, began jeering him, and ended by saying with a mocking look, that she was convinced he had only said what he did to frighten her, and that the jaguars had only existed in his imagination. Marianno gaily endured the raillery, confessed that he had perhaps displayed more anxiety than the affair deserved, and taking down a jarabe that hung on the wall, he began strumming a fandango with the back of his hand, in order to turn the conversation.

Several hours passed in laughing, talking, and singing. When the moment for departure at length arrived, Marianno went to the corral to fetch the young lady's horse, saddled it with the utmost care, and led it to the door of the rancho, after saddling his own horse, so that he might start so soon as Donna Marianna was out of sight of the rancho.

"You remained a long time in the corral,

tocayo," she said with a laugh; "pray, have you discovered any suspicious sign?"

"No, nina; but as I am also going to leave the rancho, after saddling your horse, I saddled mine."

"Of course you are going to hunt your strange jaguars again?"

"Oh, of course," he answered.

"Well," she said, with feigned terror, "if you do meet them, pray do not miss them."

"I will do all in my power to avoid that, because I desire to make you a present of their skins, in order to prove to you that they really existed."

"I thank you for your gallantry, tocayo," she replied with a laugh; "but you know the proverb: 'a hunter must not sell the skin of a—jaguar, before—'"

"Well, well, we shall soon know who is right and who wrong," he interrupted her.

The maiden, still laughing, embraced the ranchero and his wife, lightly bounded into the saddle, and bending down gracefully, offered her hand to Marianno.

"We part friends, tocayo," she said to him. "Are you coming my way?"

"I ought to do so."

"Then why not accompany me?"

"Because you would suppose, nina, that I wished to escort you."

"Ha! ha! ha!" the young lady said, merrily; "I had forgotten your proposal of this morning. Well, I hope you will be successful in your hunt; and so, good-bye till to-morrow. Come, Negro."

After uttering these words, she gave a parting wave of the hand to her nurse, and started at a gallop. The young man, after watching her for a while to be certain of the road she followed, then re-entered the rancho, took his gun, and loaded it with all the care which hunters display in this operation when they believe that life depends on the accuracy of their aim.

"Are you really about to start at once?" his mother asked him, anxiously.

"At once, mother."

"Where are you going?"

"To follow my foster-sister to the hacienda, without her seeing me."

"That is a good idea. Do you fear any danger for her?"

"Not the slightest. But it is a long distance from here to the hacienda; the Indians are moving, it is said; we are no great distance from the border, and, as no one can foresee the future, I do not wish my sister to be exposed to any chance encounter."

"Excellently reasoned, muchacho. The nina is wrong in thus crossing the forest alone."

"Poor child!" the ranchero said; "an accident happens so easily; lose no time, muchacno, but be off; on reflection, I think you ought to have insisted on accompanying her."

"You know, father, she would not have consented."

"That is true; it is better that it should be as it is, for she will be protected without knowing it. The first time I see Don Ruiz, I will recommend him not to let his sister go out thus alone, for times are not good."

But the young man was no longer listening to his father; so soon as his gun was loaded he left the rancho, followed by his dog. Two minutes later he was in the saddle, and riding at full speed in the direction taken by Donna Marianna.

So soon as the young lady found herself at a sufficient distance from the rancho, she had checked her horse's pace, which was now proceeding at an amble. It was about five in the afternoon; the evening breeze was rising, and gently waving the tufted crests of the trees; the sun, now almost level with the ground, only appeared on the horizon in the shape of a reddish globe; the atmosphere, refreshed by the breeze, was perfumed by the gentle emanations from the flowers and herbs; the birds, aroused from the heavy lethargy produced by the heat, were singing beneath all the branches, and filling the air with their joyous songs.

Donna Marianna, whose mind was impressionable, and open to all sensations, gently yielded to the impressions of this scene, which was so full of ineffable harmony, and gradually forgetting where she was and surrounding objects, had fallen into a voluptuous reverie. What was she meditating? She certainly could not have said; she was yielding unconsciously to the influence of this lovely evening and travelling into that glorious country of fancy of which life is but too often the nightmare. Donna Marianna was too young, too simple, and too pure yet to possess any memory either sad or sweet; her life had hitherto been an uninterrupted succession of sunshiny days; but she was a woman, and listened for the beatings of her heart, which she was surprised at not hearing. With that curiosity which is innate in her sex, the maiden tried with a timid hand to raise a corner of the veil that covered the future, and to divine mysteries which are incomprehensible, so long as love has not revealed them by sufferings, joy, or grief.

Donna Marianna had rather a long ride through the forest before reaching the plain; but she had so often ridden the road at all hours of the day, she was so thoroughly persuaded that no danger menaced her, that she let the bridle hang on her horse's neck, while she plunged deeper and deeper into the delicious reverie which had seized on her. In the meanwhile, the shades grew deeper; the birds had concealed themselves in the foliage, and ceased their songs; the sun had disappeared, and the hot red beams it had left on the horizon were beginning to die out; the wind blew with greater force through the branches, which uttered long murmurs; the sky was assuming deeper tints, and night was rapidly approaching. Already the shrill cries of the coyotes rose in the quebradas and in the unexplored depths of the forest; hoarse yells disturbed the silence, and announced the awakening of the savage denizens of the forest.

All at once a long, startling, strident howl, bearing some resemblance to the miawling of a cat, burst through the air, and fell on the maiden's ear with an ill-omened echo. Suddenly startled from her reverie, Donna Marianna looked up, and took an anxious glance around her. A slight shudder of fear passed over her body, for her horse, so long left to its own devices, had left the beaten track, and the maiden found herself in a part of the forest unknown to her—she had lost her way. A person lost in an American forest is dead!

These forests are generally entirely composed of trees of the same family, which render it impossible to guide oneself, unless gifted with that miraculous intuition which the Indians and hunters possess, and which enables them to march with certainty in the most inextricable labyrinths. Wherever the eye may turn, it only perceives immense arcades of verdure, infinitely prolonged, wearying the eye by their desperate monotony, and only crossed at intervals by the tracks of wild beasts, which are mixed strangely together, and eventually lead to unknown watering-places, nameless streams, that run silently and gloomily beneath the covert, and whose windings cannot possibly be followed.

The spot where the maiden was, was one of the most deserted in the forest; the trees, of prodigious height and size, grew closely together, and were connected by a network of lianas, which, growing in every direction, formed an impassable wall; from the end of the branches hung, in long festoons to the ground, that greyish moss known as Spanish beard, while the tall straight grass that everywhere covered the ground, showed that human foot had not trodden the soil here for a lengthened period. The maiden felt an invincible terror seize upon her. Night had almost completely set in; then the stories her foster-brother had told her in the morning about the jaguars returned to her mind in a flood, and were rendered more terrible by the darkness that surrounded her, and the mournful howling that burst forth on all sides. She shuddered, and turned pale as death at the thought of the fearful danger to which she had so imprudently exposed herself.

Then, collecting all her strength for a last appeal, she uttered a cry; but her voice died out without raising an echo. She was alone—lost in the desert by night. What could she do? What would become of her?

The maiden tried to find the route by which she had come, but the road followed haphazard through the herbage no longer existed—the grass trodden by her horse's hoof had sprung up again behind it. Moreover, the night was so dark that Donna Marianna could not see four paces ahead of her; and she soon found that her efforts to find the road would only result in leading her further astray. Under such circumstances, a man would have been in a comparatively far less dangerous position. He could have lit a fire to combat the night chill, and keep the wild beasts at bay; in the event of an attack, his weapons would have allowed him to defend himself: but Donna Marianna had not the means to light a fire; she had no weapons, and had she possessed them, she would not have known how to use them. She was forced to remain motionless at the spot where she was for the whole night, at the hazard of dying of cold or terror.

This position was frightful. How she now regretted her imprudent confidence, which was the cause of what was now occurring! But it was too late; neither complaints nor recrimination aught availed. She must yield to her fate. With energetic natures, however little accustomed they may be to peril, when that peril proves inevitable, and they recognise that nothing can protect them from it, a reaction takes place; their thoughts become clearer, their courage grows with their will, and they accept, with a proud and resolute resignation, all the consequences of the danger they are compelled to confront, however terrible they may be. This was what happened to the maiden when she perceived that she was really lost. A profound despair seized upon her—for a moment the weakness natural to her sex gained the upper hand, and she fell sobbing on the ground; but gradually the reaction set in, and, pious as all Spanish women are, she clasped her hands, and addressed a fervent and touching prayer to God, who was her last hope.

It has been justly said that prayer not only consoles, but strengthens and restores hope. Prayer, with those who sincerely believe, is the expression of the real feelings of the soul; only those who have looked death in the face, either on the battle-field or during a storm at sea, will understand the sublimity of prayer—the last appeal of the weak victim to the omnipotent Intelligence which can alone save him. Donna Marianna prayed, and then rose calmer, and, above all, stronger. She had placed herself in the hands of Deity, and, in her simple faith, was convinced that He would not abandon her.

Her horse, whose bridle she had not let loose, was standing motionless by her side. The maiden gently patted the noble animal, the only friend left to her; then, by a sudden inspiration, she began unfastening the girths, tearing her little hands without knowing it, and lacerating her fingers with the iron tongues of the buckles.

"Poor Negro," she said, in a soft voice, as she removed the trappings, "you must not be the victim of my imprudence; resume your liberty; for the noble instinct with which your Creator has endowed you will, perhaps, enable you to find your road. Go, my poor Negro; you are now free."

The animal gave a whinneying of delight, made a prodigious leap, and disappeared in the darkness. Donna Marianna was alone —really alone, now.

CHAPTER XXI.

STRONGHAND.

It is impossible to imagine what terrors night brings with it under its thick mantle of mist, when the earth is no longer warmed by the sparkling sunbeams, and darkness reigns as supreme lord. At that time everything changes its aspect, and assumes in the flickering rays of the moon a fantastic appearance; the mountains seem loftier, the rivers wider and deeper; the trees resemble spectres — gloomy denizens of the tomb, watching for you to pass, and ready to clutch you in their fleshless arms. The imagination becomes heated, ideas grow confused, you tremble at the fall of a leaf, at the moaning of the night breeze, at the breakage of a branch; and, suffering from a horrible nightmare, you fancy at every moment that your last hour is at hand.

In the American forests, night has mysteries still more terrible. Beneath these immense domes of verdure, which the sun it powerless to pierce even at mid-day, and which remain constantly buried in an undecided clear obscure, the darkness may, so to speak, be felt; nothing could produce a flash in this chaos, excepting, perhaps, the luminous eyeballs of the wild beasts, that dart electric sparks from the thickets. Here Night is truly the mistress; the darkness is peopled by the sinister denizens of the forest, whom the obscurity drives from their unknown hiding-places, and who begin their mournful prowling in search of prey. From each clump, from each ravine, issue confused sounds that have no name in human language; some clear and sharp, others hoarse and low, and others, again, resembling miawling, or sardonic laughter, are blended in a horrible concert. Then come the heavy footfalls on the ground, and the sullen flapping of birds' wings, as well as that incessant indistinct murmur, which is nought else but the continual buzz of the infinitely little, mingled with the hollow moan always heard in the desert, and which is only the breath of Nature travailing with her incomprehensible secrets. A night passed in the forest, without fire or weapons, is a terrible thing for a man; but the situation becomes far more frightful for a woman—a girl—a frail and delicate creature, accustomed to all the comforts of life, and unable to find within herself those thousand resources which a strong man, habituated to struggle, manages to procure, even in the most desperate situations.

Without dwelling further on the subject, the reader can imagine without difficulty the painful situation in which Donna Marianna found herself. So long as she could hear the sound of her horse's hoofs, as it fled at full speed, she stood with her body bent forward and outstretched ears, attaching herself to life, and, perchance, to hope, through the sound which was so familiar to her; but when it had died out in the distance, when a leaden silence once again weighed on her, the maiden shuddered, and, folding her hands on her chest, sank in a half-fainting condition at the foot of a tree—no longer thinking or hoping, but awaiting death. For what succour could she expect in the tomb of verdure, which, though so spacious, was not the less secure?

How long did she remain plunged in this state of prostration, which was only an anticipated death—one hour or five minutes? She could not have said. For wretched people, whom everything, even hope, abandons, time seems to stand still—minutes become ages, and an hour seems as if it would never end. All at once a feeble, almost indistinguishable sound smote her ear, and she instinctively listened. This sound grew louder with every second, and ere long she could not be mistaken; it was a rapid mad gallop through the forest. This sound Donna Marianna recognised with terror; for it was produced by the return of her horse. For the noble animal to come back with such velocity, it must be pursued, and that closely, by ferocious animals; such was Donna Marianna's idea, and, unfortunately, she only too soon recognised its correctness. The horse gave a snort of terror, which was immediately answered by two loud, sharp growls. Then, as if dreaming, Donna Marianna heard prodigious leaps; she saw ill-omened shadows pass before her with the rapidity of a lightning flash, and then a fearful struggle, in which groans of agony were mingled with yells of delight.

However terrible the maiden's position might be, she felt tears slowly course down her cheeks—her horse, her last comrade, had succumbed—the liberty she had granted it had only precipitated its destruction. Strange to say, though, at this supreme moment Donna Marianna did not think for an instant that the death of her horse probably only preceded her own by a brief space, and that it was a sinister warning to her to prepare for being devoured.

When terror has attained a certain degree, a strange effect is produced upon the individual; animal life still exists in the sense that the arteries pulsate, the heart palpitates; but intellectual life is completely suspended; the brain, struck by a temporary paralysis, no longer receives the thought; the eyes look without seeing; the voice itself cannot force its way through the contracted throat; in a word, terror produces a partial catalepsy, by destroying for a period, longer or shorter, all the noblest faculties of man. Donna Marianna had reached such a point that, even had she possessed the means of flight, she would have been incapable of employing them, so thoroughly was every feeling extinct in her—even the instinct of self-preservation, which usually remains when all the others are destroyed.

Fortunately for the girl, the jaguars—for there were several of them—were to leeward; moreover, they had tasted blood, and this was a double reason which temporarily saved her, by depriving their scent of nearly all its delicacy. No other sound was audible, save that produced by the crushing of the horse's bones, which the wild beasts were devouring, mingled with growls of anger, when one of the banqueters tried to encroach on its neighbour's share of the booty. There could be no doubt about the fact; the animals enjoying this horrible repast were the jaguars, so long hunted by the tigrero, and which her evil star had brought across the maiden's track.

By degrees, Donna Marianna became—not familiarized with the danger hanging over her head, for that would have been impossible; but as, according to the law of nature, anything that reaches its culminating point must begin to descend, her first terror, though it did not abandon her, produced a strange phenomenon. She felt involuntarily attracted towards these horrible animals, whose black outlines she could distinguish moving in the darkness; suffering from a species of vertigo, with her body bent forward, and her eyes immoderately dilated, without even accounting for the strange feeling that urged her to act thus, she kept her eyes eagerly fixed upon them, following with a febrile interest their slightest movements, and experiencing at the sight a feeling of inexplicable pleasure, which produced a mingled shudder of joy and pain. Let who will try to explain this singular anomaly of human nature; but the fact is certain, and among our readers many will, doubtless, bear witness to its truth.

All at once the jaguars, which had hitherto been greedily engaged with the corpse of the horse, without thinking of anything beyond making a hearty meal, raised their heads and began sniffing savagely. Donna Marianna saw their eyes, sparkling like live coals, fixed upon her; she understood that she was lost; instinctively she closed her eyes to escape the fascination of those metallic eyeballs, which seemed in the darkness to emit electric sparks, and prepared to die. Still the jaguars did not stir; they were crouching on the remains of the horse, and, while continuing to gaze at the maiden, gracefully passed their paws over their ears with a purr of pleasure—in a word, they were coquettishly performing their toilet, appearing not only most pleased with the meal they had just ended, but with that which was awaiting them.

Still, in spite of the calmness affected by the two animals—for the cubs were sleeping, rolled up like kittens—it was evident that for some unknown motive they were restless; they lashed the ground with their weighty tails, or laid back their ears with a roar of anger, and turning their heads in all directions, sniffed the air. They scented a danger; but of what nature was it? As for Donna Marianna, they appeared so sure of seizing her whenever they thought proper, and saw how harmless she was, that they contented themselves with crouching before her, and did not deign to advance a step. All at once the male, without stirring, uttered a sharp, quick yell. The female rose, bounded forward, seized one of her cubs in her mouth, and with one backward leap disappeared in a thicket; almost immediately she reappeared, and removed the second in the same way; then she returned calmly and boldly to place herself by the side of the male, whose anxiety had now attained formidable proportions.

At the same instant a flash traversed the air—a shot echoed far and wide—and the male jaguar writhed on the ground with a roar of agony. Almost immediately a man dashed from the tree at the foot of which Donna Marianna was crouching, stood in front of her, and received the shock of the female, which, at the shot, had instinctively bounded forward. The man tottered, but for all that kept his feet; there was a frightful struggle for a few minutes, and then the jaguar fell back with a last and fearful yell.

"Come," the hunter said, as he wiped on the grass the long machete with which he had stabbed the beast, "my arrangements were well made, but I fancy that I arrived only just in time. Now for the cubs; for I must not show mercy to any member of this horrible family."

Then this man, who seemed to possess the faculty of seeing in the darkness, walked without hesitation toward the spot where the female had hidden her cubs. He resolutely entered the thicket, and came out again almost immediately, holding a cub in either hand. He smashed their heads against the trunk of a tree, and threw the bodies on those of their father and mother.

"That is a very tidy butchery," he said; "but what on earth is Don Hernando's tigrero about, that I am obliged to do his work?"

While saying this, the hunter had collected all the dry wood within reach, struck a light, and within a few minutes a bright flame rose skywards. This duly accomplished, the stranger hurried to the assistance of Donna Marianna, who had fainted.

"Poor girl!" he muttered, with an accent of gentle pity, as he lifted her in his arms, and carried her to the fire; "how is it that the fright has not killed her?"

He gently laid her on some firs he had arranged for her bed, and gazed at her for a moment with a look of delight impossible to describe. But then he felt considerably embarrassed. Accustomed to the hardships of a desert life, and a skilful hunter as he had proved himself, this man was naturally a very poor sick-nurse. He knew how, at a pinch, to dress a wound or extract a bullet, but he was quite ignorant how to bring a fainting woman round.

"Still, I cannot leave her in this state,

poor girl," he muttered, gazing on her sorrowfully; "but what am I to do?—how can I relieve her?"

At length he knelt down by the young lady's side, gently raised her lovely head, which he laid on his knee, and opening with his dagger-point her closed lips, poured in a few drops of Catalonian refino contained in a gourd. The effect of this remedy was instantaneous. A nervous tremour passed over the maiden's body; she heaved a sigh, and opened her lips. At the first moment she looked around her wildly, but ideas seemed gradually to return to her brain; her contracted features grew brighter, and fixing her eyes on the hunter, who was still bending over her, she muttered, with an expression of gratitude which made the young man's heart beat, "Stronghand!"

"Have you recognised me, senorita?" he exclaimed, with joyous surprise.

"Are you not my Providence?" she answered. "Do you not always arrive when I have to be saved from some fearful danger?"

"Oh, senorita!" he murmured, in great embarrassment.

"Thanks! thanks, my saviour!" she continued, seizing his hand, and pressing it to her heart; "thanks for having come to my help, Stronghand, for this time again. I should have been lost without you."

"I really believe," he said, with a smile, "that I arrived just in time."

"But how is it that you came so opportunely?" she asked, curiously, as she sat up and wrapped herself in the furs, for the feminine instinct had regained its power over her.

At this question, simple though it was, the hunter turned red.

"Oh," he said, "it is very simple. I have been hunting in these parts for some days past. I had tracked this family of jaguars, which I obstinately determined to kill, I know not why; but now I understand that it was a presentiment. After pursuing them all day, I had lost them out of sight, and was seeking their trail, when your horse enabled me to recover it."

"What!—my horse?" she exclaimed, in amazement,

"Do you not remember that it was I who gave you this poor Negro on our first meeting?"

"That is true," she murmured, as she let

her eyes fall beneath the hunter's ardent glance.

"I saw you for a moment this morning, when you were going to Sanchez' rancho."

"Ah!" she remarked.

"Sanchez is a friend of mine," he continued, as if to explain his remark.

"Go on."

"On seeing the horse, which I at once recognised, I feared that some accident had happened to you, and set out after it. But the jaguars had scented it at the same time, and in spite of my thorough acquaintance with this forest, it was impossible for me to run as fast as they did. Luckily, they were hungry, and amused themselves by devouring poor Negro; otherwise I should not have arrived in time."

"But how was it that you came by this strange road?"

"In the first place, I was bound to save your life, as I knew that if I killed one jaguar, the other would leap upon you, in order to avenge it."

"But you ran the risk of being torn in pieces by the horrible animals," she said, with a shudder of retrospective terror, as she thought of the frightful dangers from which she had been so miraculously preserved.

"That is possible," he said, with an unmistakeable expression of joy; "but I should have died to save you, and I desired nothing else."

The maiden made no reply. Pensive and blushing, she bowed her head on her chest. The hunter thought that he had offended her, and also remained silent and constrained. This silence lasted several minutes. At length Donna Marianna raised her head and offered her hand to the young man.

"Thank you again!" she said, with a gentle smile. "Your heart is good. You did not hesitate to sacrifice your life for me, whom you scarce know, and I shall feel eternally grateful to you."

"I am too amply repaid for my services by these words, senorita," he replied, with marked hesitation; "still I have a favour to ask you, and I should be pleased if you would deign to grant it."

"Oh, speak, speak! tell me what I can do!"

"I know not how to explain it; my request will appear to you so strange, so singular—perhaps so indiscreet."

"Speak; for I feel convinced that the favour you pretend to ask of me is merely another service you wish to render me."

Stronghand bent a searching glance on the maiden, and then seemed to make up his mind.

"Well, senorita," he said, "it is this:— should you ever, for any reason neither you nor I can foresee, need advice or the help of a friend, either for yourself or any member of your family, do nothing till you have seen me, and explained to me unreservedly the motives that impelled you to come to me."

Donna Marianna reflected, while the hunter gazed at her attentively.

"Be it so," she at length said; "I promise to act as you wish. But how am I to find you?"

"Your foster-brother is my friend, senorita; you will request him to lead you to me, and he will do so; or, if you prefer it, you can warn me through him to proceed to any place you may point out."

"Agreed."

"I can count on your promise?"

"Have I not passed my word?"

All at once a loud noise, resembling the

passage of a wild beast, was heard in the forest glade; the maiden started, and instinctively clung to the hunter.

"Fear nothing, senorita," the latter said; "do you not recognise a friend?"

At the same moment the tigrero's dog leaped up to fondle her, followed almost instantaneously by Marianno.

"Heaven be blessed!" he said, joyfully, "she is saved!" and pressing the hunter's hand cordially, he added, "Thanks; it is a service I owe you, brother."

END OF VOL. I.

CPSIA information can be obtained
at www.ICGtesting.com
Printed in the USA
LVHW100437110522
718424LV00003B/145

9 783375 002015